"You do know I'm not getting anything out of this, right?"

No way did she believe that. "You poor thing."

He laughed, and the rich, genuine sound washed over her. So much for having the upper hand. Carter didn't seem to recognize that fact at all. He moved and it mesmerized her. He spoke and her brain replayed every word.

"I'm not my father, Hanna."

The words shook her out of her stupor because she was starting to believe him. "That's the only reason you're still standing here."

That and his eyes. And those impressive shoulders. That cool voice. Okay, she might have let him inside the shop to look at him for a while. She hadn't expected the rest.

No, Carter Jameson was not what she'd expected at all.

* * *

The Reluctant Heir is part of the Jameson Heirs series from HelenKay Dimon!

Dear Reader,

I know what it's like being the youngest child in the family. I complain because there aren't as many photos of me as there are of my elder brothers.

Carter Jameson might be rich and powerful, but his family problems run deeper than a few missing photos. There's a family business in limbo and a father who thrives on causing trouble. Carter is temporarily back, but can he stay? He's thinking no...until he sees Hanna Wilde again. She has him rethinking *everything*.

Hanna wants nothing to do with any member of the Jameson family. Her teen crush on Carter is long over, or at least she's trying hard to pretend it is. She has family problems of her own and revenge on her mind. But Carter is convincing, and he's even hotter now that he's all grown up, so it's hard to say no to his invitation to come back to Virginia. Now she just has to figure out if she can survive another round with the Jameson family.

All of this makes me think I should stop complaining about those photos...and call my mom more often.

I hope you enjoy Carter and Hanna's story!

HelenKay

HELENKAY DIMON

THE RELUCTANT HEIR

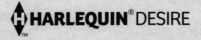

Recycling programs
for this product may
not exist in your area.

ISBN-13: 978-1-335-97175-3

The Reluctant Heir

Copyright © 2018 by HelenKay Dimon

Printed in U.S.A.

HelenKay Dimon is a divorce lawyer turned full-time author. Her bestselling and award-winning books have been showcased in numerous venues, including *The Washington Post* and *Cosmopolitan*. She is an RT Reviewers' Choice Best Book Award winner and has been a finalist for the Romance Writers of America RITA® Award multiple times.

Books by HelenKay Dimon

Harlequin Desire

The Jameson Heirs

Pregnant by the CEO
Reunion with Benefits
The Reluctant Heir

Visit her Author Profile page at Harlequin.com, or helenkaydimon.com, for more titles.

One

This could not be happening.

Hanna Wilde disconnected the call with the dry cleaner next door and stared at her cell phone.

He was here, in Milton. Many miles and a few states away from his big fancy home—make that *homes*—in the Washington, D.C. area.

Not *that* he. Not the one who'd tracked her and tried to scare her months ago. Not the one who'd threatened and lied. No, the man in her building, on his way up to her apartment, was the son, not the horrible father.

Carter Jameson. Youngest heir to a vast real estate fortune. Grandson of a disgraced congressman. The boy whose family had employed hers back when they were kids.

Her unwanted teen crush.

Amazing how the last name Jameson could start a shake running through her that rattled right down to her bones. Her reaction arose out of anger, not fear. Though, if she were being honest, she'd have to admit to a mix of both.

His visit here meant his family had hunted her down and found her again. The last round of contacts started with letters from Carter's father, Eldrick, then from his attorneys, all insisting she come in for a meeting. When she ignored those, the unwanted visits started. But she'd done what Eldrick ordered. She stayed away from Virginia and Carter and kept her mouth shut.

She'd already lost so much to the Jamesons—her father, her sister, her peace of mind. Now it looked like they were coming around again for one more shot.

She slipped her cell phone into her back jeans pocket and headed for the one closet in her studio apartment. It held her clothes, her cleaning supplies and, well, that just about constituted the entire list of what she owned. That and the photo album. If they were going to hound her it was easier to leave town for a while then go through it all again. She didn't have any real connections here anyway, but the album was coming with her. It was all she had left of the past she tried so often to forget.

The knocking started as soon as she dropped to her knees. The rickety closet door with the broken slats screeched to a halt on the tracks. She usually shoved and pushed, half lifted the thing, to get it to open the whole way. But that would make noise and require her to move, and she seemed to be frozen in place.

Her heartbeat thundered in her ears. It was the only sound in the silent room.

Then the knocking started again.

"Hello?" A deep male voice, all silky and smooth, floated through the door.

She refused to fall for that sexy sound a second time. She wasn't a teenage anymore. She knew better now…in theory. "What?"

"Hanna?"

He acted like he knew her but that had been years ago. Another time, almost another life.

"She's not here." She winced as she made the nonsensical remark.

For a second there was no response. Hanna scrambled to her feet and tiptoed to the door. She saw the shadow of Carter's feet at the bottom. So, he still stood there, quiet now.

"Are you sure you don't want to try another answer, Hanna Wilde? Maybe one a bit more believable?"

She couldn't insist he had the wrong apartment. He remembered her name and he still had the same smiling lilt to his voice. This, the guy she'd been warned to stay away from was now hanging out in the hallway. Maybe he wanted to take a turn telling her not to disclose the misdeeds of his past. Either way, she refused to be blamed for being near him when he was the one who found her.

Taking a deep breath, she threw open the front door. Almost slammed it right into her own face but had the good sense to step back in the nick of time.

Her words cut off at the sight of him. A smile lit up his stupidly handsome face. He was tall, probably six-one or so, looming over her by inches even though there was nothing tiny or petite about her.

A billionaire born into a family of extreme privilege, the type of people who did whatever they wanted, without consequence. A long line of Virginia landowners who considered themselves Southern gentlemen, a bloodline that had been broken only by a Japanese grandmother—or so said the nasty whispers of their fellow rich people. The same grandmother who had gifted Carter with the striking combination of glossy black hair and near black eyes.

Carter was the youngest of the Jameson sons. The playboy with the carefree reputation. The one not defined by the rules as much as his older brothers because no one expected or demanded anything of him. He was the "extra" child, or that was the joke his father used to describe him. She knew about the nickname because she'd watched interviews with Carter's old man, hating him as much on-screen as she had in person.

Carter had been living in California for almost a year now—after he'd breezed through her sister's life…and destroyed it.

"It's been so long." He sounded genuinely happy to see her.

Hanna ignored whatever traitorous emotion started jumping around in her stomach at the sound of his voice. "What do you want?"

"That's an interesting welcome."

She could have sworn his eyes actually sparkled. She glanced at the ceiling, figuring it had to be a trick from the hallway lighting. But no, the dude's eyes looked sunny and warm and welcoming.

This guy, the one who wined and dined her sister, made promises then left town, now acted as if nothing had happened. As if he'd lost touch with Hanna by accident, not because his father cut off all contact. He'd never really noticed her before, certainly not when she was younger and desperate for his attention, which still haunted her, but now he pretended to.

"Why are you here?" Her fingers dug into the wooden door. She held on to it like a shield, positioning her body half behind it, ready to slam it shut if he moved even an inch.

Later she would assess why just seeing him touched off a spinning inside her. Why, after all this time, her heart still sped up when he shot her an inviting look. The reaction struck her as self-destructive and wrong but realizing that didn't make it stop. It also made her wonder if she'd really overcome those feelings of not being good enough as she'd hoped.

The longer they stood there, the more those sparkly eyes dimmed. They started to narrow a bit. "Hanna? Do you remember me?"

She snorted. Little did he know she used to dream about him. "Of course."

His gaze wandered over her head, into the studio behind her. "Are you okay?"

"I was up until three minutes ago."

He let out a long, labored exhale. The kind that telegraphed a this-woman-is-working-on-my-nerves vibe. "Let's start over. My father sent me."

The memory of her youthful crush vanished. Her stomach squeezed and twisted until she had to fight the urge to yell. "To tell me to stay away? Well, I did that. If he's ticked off it's his own fault, or yours, because you came hunting me."

"What are you talking about?"

"Whatever he wants this time, the answer is no." She gave in and shoved the door. Put her weight behind it and let it fly.

Carter grabbed the edge before it crashed into his shoulder. "Whoa. What do you mean by *this time*? I have no idea what you're talking about."

Yep, his reflexes were just as solid as the rest of him. All muscle and long legs and perfect cheekbones… Man, she hated the Jameson family and their hot-male genes.

"You need to go." She'd said it in a few ways now. Maybe this time would sink in.

"What did he do? My father. Your reaction is… telling."

Carter could not be this clueless. It wasn't just his father. It was him, too. He'd created a mess and had his big ol' rich daddy sweep the problem away.

That was almost a year ago. Now Carter showed up, taking the never-happened part a bit too far. "Oh, please."

"Hanna." This time there was a bit more *oomph* behind his tone when he said her name. "We haven't seen each other in, what, ten years?"

True, and it managed to feel like both forever ago and like yesterday. "Your point?"

"Normally, I need to see a woman more often for her to be this angry with me." One eyebrow lifted. "Or can I assume my father is responsible for your mood?"

Oh, this younger Jameson was a smooth one. Calm, standing there in his slim black pants with his hands in his pockets. A short gray winter coat highlighted his trim waist and likely cost more than her beat-up car with its side view mirror held on with electrical tape.

He rocked back on his heels, as if they were having a friendly chat. She had to give him credit. Carter Jameson had never tripped through that typical gawky preteen stage. Nope, he went from young and cute back then to all grown-up and hot now. Confidence pounded off him. The mix of perfect genes and I-know-my-place-in-the-world control proved pretty compelling.

Too bad he was a lying sack of garbage.

"The threats." She stared at him, watching confusion sweep through his eyes. *Yeah, nice try.* "The baby."

The color left Carter's face. Drained away, leaving him pale and listing to one side. "Oh, damn. Please tell me you didn't date my father and get pregnant."

She almost gagged. *"What?"*

"Look…" Carter held up both hands. "He's… I don't know, charming? At least that's what women have said. I don't get it at all but—"

"Stop talking." She grabbed a handful of his jacket when her nosy neighbor from across the hall opened his door. After a quick wave to send the guy scurrying away, she pulled Carter into her apartment and shut the door, trapping them inside. Together. Which was her nightmare.

"I did not sleep with your father." She practically hissed the words at him.

"Good." Carter visibly blew out another breath as a bit of color returned to his cheeks. "You said something about a baby?"

She shouldn't have mentioned it. She refused to travel down that heartbreaking road. "How did your father find me?"

"Uh…" Carter closed one eye as if he were trying to reason something out in his head. "Were you lost?"

She didn't buy the act. This errand had a purpose and Carter was the only one of the two of them who knew what it was. "Skip to the part where you explain how and why you're here."

"Okay." His frown came and went. By the time he made eye contact again he seemed to have gotten control of whatever emotions were churning inside him. His expression morphed into a blank and unreadable one. "It's a long story, but suffice it to say, my father asked me to come and see you. Specifically, to give this to you."

He held out an envelope. Another envelope just like the ones his father had handed her and sent to her with messengers before. The idea of being told to stay away when she already had done just that didn't make any sense. But the idea of reading through more correspondence from Eldrick Jameson exhausted her. She refused to do it. She would not give him or Carter the satisfaction of ordering her around and getting their way a second time.

The envelope might as well have been on fire because there was no way she was touching it. Never again. "Put that away."

He flipped it around in the air a few times. "You don't want it?"

He sounded stunned at the thought. She almost laughed at the reaction. It was as if he didn't know his father and the old man's schemes at all. There were always strings when it came to dealing with a Jameson.

"Save us both some time and just tell me what it says."

Carter shrugged. "How should I know?"

"You're telling me you didn't open it? You flew here or took a million-dollar taxi ride or whatever and you never gave in to the itch to crack open the seal?" That seemed to defy human nature.

"Gotta say it sounds like *you* want to know what's inside." When she didn't say anything, his hand dropped. "He left the envelope for you and said he wanted you to have it. My job was to deliver it."

"Why?"

"I figured you knew."

Anger whooshed out of her, but frustration quickly settled in its place. She had no idea what was happening. From the apologetic sound of his voice, she wondered if he did either. "Are you serious? You really don't know what this assignment your father gave you is about?"

"Unfortunately, no." Carter moved around the small space, careful to dodge the corner of her dresser and the edge of her bed, to stand by the window. "I'm not sure how to ask this, so I'm just going to blurt it out. I apologize in advance for the delivery."

"That sounds ominous and—"

"Did you have a thing with my father? Maybe not sexual but…something?"

The question sounded just as horrifying the second time. The words had changed but the idea still screeched in her brain. "I don't want anything to do with your father. Never did."

"That's new."

"Meaning?"

Carter shook his head. "Well, he's been married four times and had a series of mistresses and girlfriends, so I guess some women like him."

She shivered. "I don't get that."

"On that, we agree." A smile tugged on the corner of Carter's mouth as he took a few steps around her small space.

That cocky walk, the self-assurance. The way he stepped into a room and owned it. He was older now, more attractive in the way age and life experience molded and changed a person. Defined his features. That firm chin. The sexy smile.

The teenaged version of her had suffered from a debilitating crush that made her stammer and stare at her feet during the few times he'd talked to her. The grown-up version of her, the one who had experienced nothing but grief and anguish at the hands of the Jameson family, appreciated the way he looked but was smart enough to be wary. To not get reeled in.

"So, your father's sole instructions were to find me and give me that."

"Yes." He held the envelope out again.

None of this made sense. She'd never said anything. Never tried to see Carter. Ripped up the damn check his father had given her as a payoff, but there's no way the elder and famously impulsive Mr. Jameson had waited all these months to send Carter to try to pay her off again. Something else was happening here.

A terrible thought floated through her mind, freezing her to the spot by the door. "Is he with you?"

"My father?" Carter shook his head. "He's not even in the country, as far as I know. He and the new wife live in Tortola. Since I haven't heard from him in a few weeks, I'm assuming he's back there."

She noticed Carter didn't sound upset about living that many miles apart. The family dysfunction was his business, but she did have a few seconds of silent celebration at the thought of being some distance away from Carter's father. "Good."

Carter eyed her, his gaze assessing her, as he leaned against the wall next to the window. "I'm guessing whatever happened between you two was bad."

"The good news is you've done your duty. Daddy asked you to visit me and you did. Mission accomplished." It was time for Carter to leave. She needed to make plans, figure out where she went from here.

"I still have the envelope, so I'm not convinced we've resolved anything."

"The reality is I'm not related to the man, so I don't have to do what he wants."

Carter made a noise that sounded a bit like *huh* before he started talking. "Any chance you're going to fill in the blanks and tell me what all of this is about?"

No way would she give up her small advantage by sharing anything she knew. "Hey, stud. You came to see me."

"I guess shy little Hanna is all grown-up now."

She reached out and opened the door. "And she's done with this conversation."

He pushed off from the wall and took the few steps that put him in front of her. "You know this isn't over, right?"

Her hand tightened on the doorknob. "Sure feels like it."

His smile returned as he nodded. "Goodbye for now, Hanna."

Then he was in the hall and she slammed the door behind him. Her heart hammered in her chest as she tried to drag in enough air to breathe. She gulped and panted as she fell against the door, letting her back slide down when her knees gave out and she fell to the floor in a boneless heap.

"Now what?"

Carter walked out of the lobby and stepped into the cold upstate New York evening. Winter fell early and heavy here. There was talk of snow in the forecast and he wanted to be long gone before it arrived.

It was a little after five. The sun had set and clouds filled the darkening sky. He zipped his jacket to block some of the biting October wind. He glanced up at Hanna's window and saw a peek of light behind the drawn curtains blocking his view inside.

She might not want to reminisce with him, but he possessed some vivid memories of her. Shy and pretty. She'd been a teenager on his family's Virginia estate and had hidden behind her older, more outgoing sister. The Wilde girls. Back then he'd thought of himself and Hanna as friends. It wasn't until he was older that he'd realized he'd held the sisters at a distance. He'd all but ignored Hanna, treating her as the child of the "help" and nothing more, just as his father insisted.

Carter shook his head, hating the reminder of his past and who he'd once been. The same history he'd run from and gotten dragged back into when his brother called him home, asking for help. Now Carter was the one who needed assistance. At the very least, a little information. He couldn't do much more without that.

He grabbed his cell phone out of his jacket pocket and called Jackson Richards, the real hub of information at Jameson Industries and one of the few people in the world Carter actually liked and trusted.

"Hey, I need your help."

"Nothing new there. You still working on your top-secret mission for your dad?"

Carter decided to ignore the question as he listened to Jackson typing in the background. "Ready for the list?"

"Wait, don't you have an assistant?"

"I don't actually work at the company. I'm happy staying on the Virginia property, far away from the family business."

Carter's preference for the Virginia countryside was a fact his father had once used to drive a wedge between Carter and his brothers. They were the business-minded ones. He was the disappointment. Carter had heard the refrain so often it rang in his ears even now.

He'd come back to the D.C. area expecting to check in on his brothers and help out with their on-going fight with their dad about governing interest in the business, then go again. When that didn't happen he'd settled in to the Virginia estate. It was a small act of defiance against his father, who had kicked him out of that same property almost a year ago and told him never to come back.

But now he needed some intel. "No one is as good at this stuff as you are."

"Flattery won't work." Jackson cleared his throat. "For the record, expensive liquor will."

"Done. As soon as I get back, I'll come by with a bottle." Carter moved out of the glare of the streetlight and leaned against the brick wall of Hanna's apartment building. Cars buzzed by and people moved around him on the sidewalk, likely on their way to the bars and restaurants two blocks over. "I need all the information you can get me on Hanna and Gena Wilde. Sisters. Their dad used to work for our family at our Virginia estate."

"Do you know what you sound like when you say *estate* like that?"

"I have an idea." Carter glanced at his watch and made a quick decision. "You have three hours to gather intel."

The typing stopped. "What the hell? I do have a real job, you know."

A fair argument but a strange anxious feeling settled inside Carter. He sensed if he didn't talk to Hanna again soon, this time armed with information, she'd slip away. And he didn't want to go another ten years without seeing her again.

The wary blue eyes, almost baby blue. That wavy, shoulder-length, deep auburn hair that he ached to run his fingers through. The way her jeans balanced on her hips, giving him the tiniest glimpse of bare pale stomach as the edge of her long-sleeve T-shirt shifted around. He wanted to know more. To talk with her. To dig and see what had her on edge.

He guessed he'd trace most of her problems right back to his father. Carter had no idea what had her spooked or what game his father was playing, but something bigger than an envelope was happening here.

Carter took it out and studied it. No writing or clue to the contents. It was killing him not to rip it open. If he didn't have an answer in a few days, he would. Until then, he could respect her privacy…but barely.

Jackson sighed into the phone. "Does this have something to do with your highly problematic father?"

"Doesn't everything? Talk to you soon."

Carter hung up before Jackson could complain or swear. He glanced up at Hanna's studio a second time. "It looks like I'm not going anywhere just yet."

Two

Hanna decided to get away. Not forever. Just long enough for the Jamesons to find another target. Her job was a temporary solution anyway. She cleaned houses and businesses. Worked part-time in the coffee shop. She could take time off but she had to do it without pay, which sucked. That choice would be a financial struggle but going round and round with the Jamesons could cost her the equilibrium she'd been fighting to gain ever since her sister's death.

For the hundredth time, Hanna wondered if she should have just taken the money Eldrick offered her months ago to stay away from Carter. She'd tried to find Carter back then, and then the stay-away letters started. Then came the bribe.

The cash would have made rebuilding her life much easier. Saying no just made Eldrick double down on the threats of attorneys and lawsuits if she came near his family or talked about them with anyone. He thought it was her job to keep his family secrets.

Man, she hated the Jamesons and how they turned everything upside down. Irrational or not, that hate extended to all Jamesons…even, admittedly to a lesser degree, to the one she used to stare at as he played football on the lawn with his brothers. The one who turned her into a babbling fool every time he smiled at her.

Back then, of course. She was wiser now.

She dunked the mop in the murky water with a bit too much force. The wheels under the bucket spun around. Before she could catch it, the bucket tumbled and smacked into the coffee counter, sending the dirty water spilling over the sides.

Apparently, it was going to be that kind of day.

She sighed as she balanced the mop handle against the edge of the counter and wiped her hands on her faded blue jeans. A tingle at the base of her neck had her glancing up and turning around. The shadow moved in the glass front door of Morning Grind, the coffee shop she cleaned to offset part of the cost of her rent upstairs. Her breath hitched as the face came into view.

Carter.

Of course it was.

It was five in the morning and still dark outside, but she could see every inch of that amazing face. Watch his shoulders lift as he shifted his weight from foot to foot, likely trying to fight off the punishing cold that had settled in early this year, or so the locals told her.

She should let him freeze. Let him form a big Jameson ice cube right there on the sidewalk.

So tempting. But that would just give his father a reason to breeze into town, blaming and threatening her about something new.

She wiped her hands on her jeans again. This time not to dry them off but to beat down the nerves jumping around inside her. A strange mix of wariness and excitement hit her the second Carter pinned her with a crooked smile.

No wonder her sister had gotten reeled in. If the gossip site stories about him were true, a lot of women had trouble saying no to the guy.

Maybe the whole turning-otherwise-smart-women-into-giant-puddles-of-goo thing was an inherited skill. A family trait of some sort. If so, she needed to get over the affliction and fast.

Her hand shook as she turned the lock and opened the door a fraction. "What?"

"You need to work on your welcoming tone." He grumbled something under his breath before talking at normal volume again. "I was hoping you'd be a bit happier to see me this morning."

"Since you seem determined to stalk me, no. For the record, I'm not into that." Or being unsure or off-kilter or vulnerable. None of those feelings worked for her, even though they all raced through her now as she tried not to notice how the wind brought a sexy rush of color to his cheeks.

"I wanted to apologize for just dropping in on you last night."

Sure he did. "By dropping in on me this morning."

The corner of his mouth lifted even higher, showing off that arresting smile. "Now that you mention it, I guess this visit wasn't all that well thought-out either."

She studied him, letting her gaze wander over that mouth before giving him full-on eye contact. The cute, self-deprecating act held a certain charm, but she knew it was just an act. No longer a carefree boy, he was a man who possessed power and money. In her experience, the Jamesons used both of those as a weapon against others.

Then there was the more obvious problem. "How did you know where to find me at this time of the morning?"

His mouth opened and closed twice.

She cleared her throat. "I'm waiting."

"Yeah, I can see that."

She knew stalling when she heard it. Heck, she excelled at that sort of thing. He couldn't fool her. "Feel free to use words."

He made a strangled noise that sounded like *hmm.* "I'm going to be honest with you."

"That would be nice." Not that she'd believe whatever he said, but it would be interesting to see what subterfuge he tried to use on her.

He unzipped his coat, just enough for her to see the V-neck of the blue sweater underneath. "I had a friend back at the Jameson office look into you."

Look into? Creative word choice. "You mean, investigate me."

"I didn't say that."

That was kind of her point. "So, you had one of your employees *not* investigate me."

"I don't actually work for Jameson Industries."

"Uh-huh." It was as if he didn't know his own last name or for some reason thought the verbal gymnastics would work on her. Either way, she wasn't buying it. "I often call up places where I don't work and get people to scurry around, looking stuff up for me in the middle of the night."

"It does seem to lack credibility when you say it that way."

"Is there another way to say it?"

She hated to admit that she was enjoying this steady back-and-forth that had her mind clicking.

After months of reeling and mourning, she still kept to herself, not letting anyone she met move past the acquaintance stage and into the friend stage. Not dating. She blamed her time away from the friendship and dating pool as the reason for the adrenaline surging through her now.

Not a new round of attraction. Nope, that could not happen.

"I called in a favor, but that's not the point." He held up a hand when she started to respond. "Initially, I assumed coming here and handing you an envelope would get the job done. When it became clear that wasn't going to happen, I decided I needed to know more about you."

She folded her arms in front of her. "Because that's not heavy-handed at all."

"I *wanted* to know more about you. About who you are now." With that, his eyes wandered—not far and not too obvious—but he did give her a quick once-over.

She hated that her stomach tumbled in response. She vowed to ignore the effect seeing him after all this time still had on her. The weird bubbling giddiness, the feeling of not being good enough or pretty enough. All those sensations she'd felt as a teen still battled inside her, which she found truly ridiculous. Getting older should have made her immune to him and all those stupid insecurities.

Guilt swamped her. He'd abandoned her sister and her own failure to stick up for Gena, to hold the line and not feel anything for him, was nothing short of a betrayal to her sister. Gena had talked about Carter leaving and his father sniffing around, trying to figure out what Carter had meant to her. She'd warned Hanna to be careful and not trust them.

Hanna tried to hold on to all of that advice and mistrust, to funnel what had been her sister's pain and her own frustration, into a defensive shield against Carter. To question every word he said and bury that leftover attraction down deep, but it kept bubbling back to the surface.

Some of the lightness left his face. "You've changed."

The words and his seemingly innocent delivery had her anger spiking. Heat raged through her. After all those years of ignoring her, he pretended he had some insight into her then and now. "Did we know each other well enough for you to make that assessment?"

"I remember the Hanna who would run around the Virginia property and get into everything. Climbing fences and trying to play on the equipment." He shoved his hands in his dark gray jeans pockets and focused that intense stare on her.

She didn't flinch. "You mean the same Virginia property I wasn't allowed to visit after my dad died?"

His eyes narrowed. "What?"

Years before Hanna lost her sister, she lost her father. Her parents had long been divorced but her mom had been listed as her father's heir and tried to go to the cottage he lived in on the Jameson estate. Her mother never talked about what happened during the visit, but she came back with clothes and a few personal items and that was all.

Hanna knew more existed. Her father had kept a journal. He'd been a faithful employee at the estate for decades. He'd built a life there, had friends and people who worked for him and respected him.

He died on the job at that stupid Virginia estate and her mother had gotten excuses and two duffel bags filled with dirty shirts.

Carter shrugged. "Okay. Visit Virginia now."

He seemed as surprised to have said the words as she'd been to hear them. "Sure, I'll just use the key I don't have and go into the house I'm not allowed to visit in the state I don't live in."

"Maybe the envelope is an invitation to visit."

"You think after all this time your father is willing to hand over my father's property and wrote to tell me?"

"I can't explain my father's actions, but I can offer to help now. If you don't want anything to do with him or the envelope, then deal with me. Come back to Virginia and get whatever you need."

Temptation tugged at her. She could go to the property and maybe get some answers to all those questions about her father's death. About how a man so skilled could fall off a ladder and die. But that meant trusting Carter and possibly running in to Eldrick. It meant owing them, and she'd vowed never to do that.

Breaking eye contact, Carter glanced around. His gaze moved over the tables with the chairs stacked on the tops, and the shelves of merchandise. It hesitated on the espresso machine. "You must have vacation days."

If he'd looked into her background, he already knew the answer. But, fine. They could play this game.

"I'm not a full-time employee." She lifted her chin because she was not going to hide who she was or what she did to earn a living. "I clean houses and buildings. It's what I do so that I can eat."

"Sure. Okay."

"Sometimes I also take shifts here, usually nights and weekends when the college kids who work here would rather go out."

He shrugged again. "Makes sense."

The casual acceptance threw her off. He came from inconceivable wealth. Growing up he only ran with other kids from the same background. He'd segregated himself as if money did matter. Went to a private boys' school, then off to an expensive college. Spent the last year playing in California. She knew because his photo showed up on gossip sites now and then with this beautiful woman or that one on his arm. And it always pricked at her.

"I'm not ashamed of what I do." She wanted to be absolutely clear about that.

"You shouldn't be."

Okay, he said that but nothing in his past or looking at him now suggested he actually believed it. "I work hard. I don't get to play much, and I certainly can't just hop off to Virginia."

"Then open the envelope."

He made it sound so simple, but it wasn't.

"Your father is trying to manipulate me. He's done it before. Sends letters and expects me to jump to his commands." And she had…sort of. When she'd emerged from the fog surrounding her sister's death she'd made a promise. She would never again let Eldrick intimidate or scare her. That meant not letting him in to her life. Not letting him in her door or reading his letters.

Carter sighed. "Tell me why and I can try to help."

"No." Part of her still believed Carter knew and this was some sort of game. He was the one who had a relationship with Gena. He'd lured her in with promises of a future then left. Everything that came after—the threats and bribery attempts by Eldrick—related back to Carter. How could he not know?

But that expression seemed so genuine. The offer of coming to Virginia opened a door she'd thought she'd closed. The possibilities whirled around in her head until she had to lean against one of the tables.

"I'm staying at the Virginia estate, so I can pack up whatever may belong to your dad and get it to you. Or, hear me out." Carter held up a hand. "Come to Virginia yourself. Get whatever property, whatever closure, you need."

She snorted. It came out before she could stop it. "Because you know so much about closure."

"I've been hunting for it for years where my father is concerned. If I can't find it for me, maybe I can at least hope you get it." A new emotion moved into his eyes. Behind that determination something else lingered. A note of sadness, maybe. "My father isn't in the country. My brothers don't go to our estate except for special events. I'm there, but I'll stay out of your way."

The idea of taking a look at her father's possessions, of figuring out once and for all if something else happened that sunny afternoon when he died, tugged and pulled at her. But the offer also tripped the silent alarm in her head. The internal warning wail almost had her wincing.

"I can't just walk away from my responsibilities." *Like some people.*

"You're not the only one who is sick of my father's constant maneuvering." Carter hesitated for a few seconds before continuing. "I can help you with whatever he wants from you, but if you don't want that I still can make sure you get access to the house you once lived in. Stay a few days and do what you need."

Common sense battled with curiosity. She'd never bought the story about her dad's death. Being there might let her take a peek and move on…or she could uncover the truth, and she owed her dad that.

But there was still the problem of the newest envelope and whatever Eldrick intended to threaten her about now. "What makes you think your father wants something? I know why I think it, but what do you know?"

"The man doesn't make a move without an ulterior motive." Carter shook his head. "Look, the easiest thing to do would be to open the envelope. But it's your life, not mine. You want to keep your secrets? Fine."

He actually sounded like he *did* get it. That eased some of the tension zipping through her.

"I don't want to be manipulated by my father either. Honestly, I'm only here because my brother, you probably remember Derrick, only gets the family business if certain conditions are met. My brothers have a list of things we must do for that inheritance to happen and this is what I have to do."

She didn't like that at all. "You mean me. I'm your 'thing to do.' How flattering."

Carter frowned. "I don't really understand why or what any of this means or how you fit in, which is likely how my dad wanted it."

He didn't exactly speak about his father with love and respect. That piqued her interest, made her want to ask questions, but she refrained. Getting sucked into a big Jameson family mess was not on her agenda today…or ever. "So, you need me to open the envelope."

"I don't need anything. My brother does. But if Derrick had seen the look of panic on your face last night when I mentioned Dad, Derrick would have torn up the envelope and told you to never worry about any of us again."

If true, she liked Derrick way more now than she

did when she was a kid and was kind of afraid of him. "And you?"

"We both know you and my dad have unfinished business of some sort." When she started to deny it, he interrupted her again. "I'm not asking what it is, but I'm giving you a chance to do some exploring on your own, without his knowledge or interference. To come back to his home turf of Virginia and figure it all out, then decide if you want to confront my dad."

She never wanted to see the man again. She'd tucked away in this corner of New York, far away from the bribery and warnings specifically to avoid having to see him. "What do you get out of all of this?"

"Honestly?" He winced. "The idea of going behind my dad's back and letting you on the property where he didn't want you to be gives me an odd satisfaction. Plus, I liked your dad. You deserve to go through his things and visit the place you stayed one last time."

"You sort of sound reasonable." Which immediately made her skeptical.

Carter took in a long, deep breath. "My offer is for housing and food, if you want it."

So smooth. He knew exactly what to say to get her thinking. There was no way he could have guessed from his investigation into her background that there were doubts swirling in her head about that Virginia estate and what really happened to her father there. This offer might be her one chance to look around without a bunch of people following her or chasing her off the property. She might be able to uncover the truth.

The only problem? Nothing ever turned out to be free.

"Who did you say would be at the property?" Not that she was conceding. This was all part of a big plan Carter's dad had worked out. She was sure of it and equally determined not to be a pawn. But if she could get the upper hand, then maybe...

"I'll be in the main house. I'm living and working there."

Her stupid heart jumped. She had no idea why that deep voice affected her. She should know better, learn from her sister's mistakes. "I thought you didn't work for the family."

His head dipped to the side for a second. "It's a complicated story."

"It always is." Because there was nothing easy about the Jameson family.

"Does this mean you're coming back with me?"

He looked far too satisfied with himself. That didn't sit right with her at all. She had the sense that once Carter thought he'd won, he would become impossible.

"I didn't say that."

He smiled. "You kind of did."

That look. His face. It was so handsome it bordered on annoying. "You leave and I'll think about the offer."

"Not exactly a people person, are you?"

Not the first time she'd heard that. She'd been tagged as the quiet sister. Not as pretty or outgoing or charismatic but steady. She got a little tired of playing the role of forgotten sister.

She'd grown up and grown apart from Gena.

Hanna moved away and worked as an administrative assistant. Had a good job. Friends. A life. When Gena's world came crashing down after Carter, she'd begged for help and Hanna came rushing in. She pushed aside the mix of jealousy and hurt that swamped her at the idea of Gena and Carter together when Gena had known all about the old crush. But she'd arrived too late to save her sister. Even now as she tried to rebuild her life and find a job to replace the one she'd lost, the guilt over not doing enough or the right thing still beat down on her every day.

He rocked back on his heels. "You do know I'm not getting anything out of this, right?"

No way did she believe that. "You poor thing."

His gaze slipped back to the espresso machine. "I'd settle for something with caffeine in it."

"You could open a bag and suck on a bean."

He laughed and the rich, genuine sound washed over her. He moved and it mesmerized her. He spoke and her brain replayed every word.

"I would have been disappointed if you'd offered to make me coffee," he said.

"I'm happy we understand each other." She glanced at the clock and dread pummeled her. Employees would start showing up in about fifteen minutes and she still had to deal with that puddle on the floor. "I need to get back to work."

"Here." Without another word, Carter went over the counter and grabbed the mop. "I can take care of the spill."

She would have been less surprised if he'd made a cup of coffee magically appear in his hand. "You're going to clean something? You…?"

"I have skills."

She could feel her mouth drop open and her eyes bulge. "With a mop?"

"I'm not my father, Hanna."

The words shook her out of her stupor because she was starting to believe him. "That's the only reason you're still standing here."

That and his eyes. And those impressive shoulders. That cool voice. Okay, she might have let him inside the shop to look at him for a while. She hadn't expected him to offer a way for her to settle the past.

No, Carter Jameson was not what she expected at all. Problem was she didn't have a defense against this Carter and that made him potentially more dangerous to her than Eldrick.

Three

Carter walked into Jackson's Jameson Industries office two days later without knocking. Since he carried sandwiches and everything else they needed for lunch, Carter doubted Jackson would mind the unscheduled intrusion.

He'd volunteered to pick up the food because he needed a distraction from his phone and its lack of messages.

There was exactly one reason for his frustration: Hanna. She still hadn't gotten in touch with him. No call. No message. No text. He'd made a point of giving her his contact information after making his big come-to-Virginia offer, convinced she wouldn't refuse…and yet, nothing.

The hours ticked by and he tried to forget her and their odd meeting, write off her apparent mix of disdain and disinterest. Not dwell on the secrets she hid and her relationship, whatever it was, to his father. Not think about how she'd grown up, about her legs or the gentle sway of her hips as she'd tried to rush him out her door. That face. Those curves.

Yeah, he definitely needed to find something else to think about.

Carter glanced up as he shut the office door behind him. Jackson sat at his desk, studying the contents of the file with such extreme concentration that it looked as if he expected to be tested on the details. Carter got three steps across the room before Jackson started talking. He didn't lift his head but his voice rang out loud and clear.

"Are you ever going to tell me why you needed the information?" Jackson asked while flipping pages.

Carter froze in midstep. "Did we start a conversation before I entered the room? Because I have no idea what you're talking about."

With a long, exaggerated sigh, Jackson finally lifted his head. After a quick look up and down, he frowned. It was the kind of once-over Jackson did before he launched into a Jamesons-are-impossible speech. The same kind of look that made Carter self-conscious, and he was rarely that.

After the prolonged visual inspection, Jackson rested his elbows on the desk in front of him. "The Wilde sisters."

"Oh, right." Knowing this topic could lead to trouble, Carter tried to deflect. A shrug usually worked, so he went with that. "That was nothing."

"Uh-huh." Jackson closed the file almost in slow-motion before lounging back in his big leather seat. "I've worked for this family for years. I've investigated many people and businesses. It's never *nothing* and it usually causes trouble that rolls downhill to my desk to fix."

Carter started to shrug a second time, then stopped because Jackson would notice multiple shrugs and take it as a sign of…something. "I just wondered what happened to them."

"Right. So, your dad sends you on this errand. You go and while you're there you just happen to need emergency intel on the daughters of the man who used to be the caretaker of your family's Virginia property. A man who died on the job, though you know that part."

Carter dropped the bag filled with food on the edge of the desk and sat down across from Jackson. "See? Perfectly reasonable."

"That's not a word I would ever use to describe your family."

The bag rustled, making a crinkling sound, as Carter unloaded the sandwiches and what looked to him like two child-sized bags of chips. "Do people really only eat seven chips at a meal?"

He threw one of the bags in Jackson's general direction. Instead of catching it, Jackson stayed still. The chips crunched as they landed on his keyboard. The only reaction he gave was the slight lift of an eyebrow. Carter took that to mean Jackson was not ready for a new topic.

"So, when you asked me about Hanna and Gena— and yes, I remember their names because I remember everything—that was just a coincidence?" Jackson asked.

"I sense you're not going to let this go."

"Want me to give you a list of all of the other people who worked at the Virginia property?" Jackson ripped open the bag of chips and shoved two in his mouth.

The room filled with the sounds of munching, shuffling and sandwich unwrapping. But Carter knew it was only a brief reprieve. Jackson had an annoying habit of holding on to a question and unloading it later, just when Carter relaxed his guard. "It's kind of freaky how much you know about our family."

"I like to be ready."

"For?"

Jackson handed over one of the two water bottles sitting by his phone. "Anything. It's a good trait in an employee, so feel free to give me a raise."

"If I had that power, I would." Hell, he'd sign over part of his interest in the company and bolt. The day-to-day monotony of desk work didn't appeal to him. And being here reminded him that his father thought he wasn't worthy to even have an office.

If Derrick didn't need him and if his sister-in-law-to-be Ellie's pregnancy eased into a safer rhythm, he might. Of course, then he'd miss seeing what would happen as his other brother, Spence, tried to negotiate a new stage of his relationship with his fiancée, Abby. And that was just too funny to miss.

Poor Spence had it bad and Abby was not the type to make it easy for him. Carter loved her for that. Loved both of the women his brothers managed to convince to date them. They were smart, beautiful and strong. Very different from each other, but perfect for Derrick and Spence.

Which for some reason got Carter thinking about Hanna. She had the smart, beautiful and strong combination down. She also looked at him like she wanted to backhand him with a mop handle, so it was good he wasn't interested. Not in anything permanent anyway. There was no way to have a few private, discreet hookups just for fun with his family nearby. Someone always seemed to be watching. And sometimes it was the guy sitting right in front of him.

Jackson. Friend, invaluable asset to Jameson Industries and all-around smart-ass.

"Stop acting like you're not management." Jackson finished unwrapping the sandwich and crumpled the paper underneath it. "You could write me a check tomorrow. In fact, you should. You know, just because."

Carter knew Jackson was kidding but he'd hit on a sore spot. One Carter couldn't exactly laugh off since it guided everything he'd done for the last year. "My father ran me out of the family and the business a year ago, remember? No power to do anything here."

Jackson swallowed the bite he'd been chewing. "When did you get so dramatic?"

"You weren't here, but he did." Carter grabbed for his food. He fiddled with the paper, trying to untuck the edge, but finally gave in and ripped it open. The smell of tuna fish salad hit him a second later.

"I missed the actual office fight between you two, but I do remember the fallout. You refused to talk. Derrick was pissed because your dad refused to listen to your ideas about what to do with the Virginia property." Jackson shook his head as he whistled. "It was a hell of a welcome back from my vacation."

"I believe the exact phrase Dad used was that my ideas were *beneath the Jameson name.*" The dismissive tone echoed in Carter's brain. No matter how he tried to write off his father and erase the memory, it kicked up every now and then. "He pointed out that I was an embarrassment and should go out and prove myself or not bother to step in his office again."

"That is some interesting Jameson tough love." Jackson took another bite, almost devouring half the sandwich in only a few minutes.

Carter glanced at the tuna fish, then to his unopened bag of chips. The idea of food suddenly didn't appeal to him. He blamed the office and the city. Being this close to what his father viewed as the center of his power made Carter want to be anywhere else. To not be a Jameson or have to deal with the steady stream of disappointing everyone. It was easier to be away and just be Carter, not the rich kid who didn't live up to the family standard.

He dropped the sandwich and then pushed the paper away from him. "He deactivated my key card to the building and told security to kick me out that afternoon. Derrick undid the orders, or so he said when he called and asked me to come back, but I was done by then."

"Eldrick couldn't make a phone call without having three people help him." Jackson swore under his breath. Not that he was quiet about it or tried to hide his anger at Eldrick. "But yeah, that will teach me to take three days of vacation. By the time I got back you were driving across the country and the office had descended into chaos."

Jackson's controlled outburst eased some of the frustration coursing through Carter. There was something comforting about having Jackson on his side that made talking about his father tolerable. "Your timing was terrible. You take three days off a year and you picked *those* days."

Jackson did what he often did when talking about family business: he shook his head. "All kidding aside, your father is an ass."

Among other things. "Very true."

"You have a second chance, you know." Jackson made a show of taking a drink and wiping his hands on his napkin. Drew out the suspense but didn't deliver a punch line.

Carter didn't shy away from asking. "Meaning?"

"Derrick liked your ideas about converting the Virginia property. He had me look into the legalities of changing the property's legal use and run some numbers on the financial feasibility of trying your solution."

For the business retreat and possible private club and party event facility? That was news to Carter. *"What?"*

"Like you, Derrick doesn't often agree with your father. He has always been pretty clear that his memories of living at the estate as a kid weren't great."

"It was fine, if you liked yelling." Carter thought about the big redbrick mansion, stately with the columns surrounded by acres of rolling hills. The pool, the pond, the outbuildings. As much as he loved the house and the outdoors and the open space, it was hard to ignore the bad memories that lingered over every inch of the land.

He'd been a teenager when his mother got cancer. Only a few months older than that when she went into the hospital, then to hospice to live out her final days, where Dad served her with divorce papers. Eldrick couldn't allow her the simple dignity of dying in peace. No, he thought his girlfriend was pregnant and he needed to move on. His girlfriend wasn't and now he was on wife number four and Carter doubted the man was one ounce more faithful to this one than he had been to Carter's mother.

Before his mother's death and the shock and the ripping sensation of having all his safety nets stripped away, life hadn't been so great either. Dad used his wife and sons as public props while bouncing between ignoring them and screaming at them in private. He was demanding and difficult and manipulative. He liked to pit Derrick and Spence against each other. It was a miracle the brothers managed to maintain any meaningful sibling relationship, let alone establish the strong one they had.

As soon as he graduated, Carter escaped and shuffled off to college, only visiting when ordered home, which amounted to little more than once a year at the holidays. Even when Derrick had moved back home with the thought of taking over the family business, he'd skipped the mansion and moved to D.C. Insisted the commute to the office would be prohibitive, which was true but not really the reason he avoided the place.

As the years rolled by, the brothers rarely used the space for weekend getaways or events. For the most part, the big house and the grounds stood empty. El-drick lived there on and off, depending on whether his then girlfriend or wife, or whomever he was sleeping with at the time, had any interest in the country.

A skeleton staff ran the place. The only event Carter could remember attending there in the last few years was Derrick and Ellie's engagement party. Ellie had insisted the party would replace some of the bad memories of growing up there with good memories. It was a nice thought, but Carter didn't think it had worked.

"Which is why you should repurpose the house and grounds." Jackson tipped the small bag and dumped the remaining chips and crumbs on his desk blotter. "Talk to Derrick. Of course, all of this de-pends on if you intend to stick around."

The tone. Jackson might not be related to them, but he shared Derrick's ability to convey a get-your-act-together message with a few words.

"Are you trying to lure me back into the family?" For the first time in a long time, Carter entertained the idea and it was all due to his brothers. The idea of fitting in, of being a part of something that didn't depend on his father's whims, appealed to him even though he was not a set-down-roots kind of guy. But maybe he could let something matter to him. Maybe.

Jackson picked up a chip and pointed it at Carter. "Forget your dad. You and your brothers support each other. I understand how that works because it's how it is with me and Zoe."

"Ah, yes." Carter smiled at the thought of Jack-son's fraternal twin. She looked like him with brown hair and blue eyes, only female and much prettier. Petite and fiery. She was one of the most determined people Carter had ever met. "Your baby sister. You are eight minutes older, right?"

Jackson's mouth flatlined. "Pretend I don't have a sister."

"But I love her." Like the sister he never had, but Carter didn't say that part out loud. Not when he enjoyed Jackson's reaction to the joke of potentially tying him even more tightly to the Jamesons through his sister's dating choices.

"Get over it," Jackson said in his most grumbly voice.

The fact was, they all viewed Jackson and Zoe as family. And some days, when his resistance was down, Jackson admitted that the feeling was mutual. Well, one time he had. He'd gotten drunk one New Year's Eve and let that slip. Now he denied it.

Carter decided to take pity on Jackson. "You do know if I made a pass Zoe would kick me in the balls, right?"

Jackson snorted. "Who do you think taught her that move?"

"Figures."

Jackson grabbed the chip bag in front of Carter and opened it, dipping his fingers inside. "But back to the Virginia house. I'm telling you that when Derrick is in charge—and I'm hoping that happens soon because I dread the idea of Eldrick dropping back into the office again—you should run it by him. You might be surprised by how much support you get."

"Is there anything you don't know about this family and the business?"

"Nope." Jackson popped one of Carter's chips in his mouth.

"We're lucky to have you."

Jackson stopped chewing long enough to smile. "That's what I keep telling you all."

She should run and keep running.

That thought raced through Hanna's mind as she stepped out of the cab she really couldn't afford in front of a gate meant to keep her out. She stared up at the high wall that circled and protected the James-ons' expansive Virginia property. This was how rich people lived—cut off from others, safe from having to touch or talk with anyone but their own.

For years, on and off, she'd lived behind that wall when she visited her father during those weekends, school holidays and a handful of weeks in the sum-mer when he had visitation. During those times, she'd slip through the gate. Not this one, of course. The one around the side meant for staff. Never really wel-come or accepted inside, her presence had been toler-ated so long as she stayed quiet and knew her place.

Despite all the rules, her father insisted he enjoyed working here because he was part of something. That living at the estate, having the responsibility of man-aging the grounds, gave him purpose. He'd felt at home there.

He'd also died there.

That's why she'd taken Carter's suggestion and showed up. Before they talked, she'd convinced her-self she needed to move on and rebuild. Not look to the past. But now the need for answers gnawed at her. Real ones, not the ones passed through Eldrick's fancy lawyers years ago. For the first time since she lost Gena, Hanna felt like she might be able to control some part of her life.

Her mother had collected the death benefit check along with Eldrick's short explanation. After years of fighting over custody schedules with her father, when it came to his death, her mother mourned. She also never believed the Jameson line about Dad falling off a ladder. Neither did Hanna.

Standing there, lost in a haze of memories, she heard the rumble and crunch of tires. She watched a dark sedan slow down as it drove by. The driver stared at her, and at the scuffed duffel bag with the broken strap sitting at her feet. She stared right back, watching until the car turned a corner and headed for one of the other estates that dotted the hillside.

"I hate being here." She mumbled the truth to herself as she slipped her cell out of her front jeans pocket. Her finger hesitated over Carter's number just as it had every time she started to call over the last few days.

She'd shown up unannounced, but she first called the Jameson office in D.C. pretending to be a business contact looking for him. The person who answered said he wasn't there, so she took a shot that he'd been telling the truth when he said he lived and worked at the estate now.

It was just one of many chances she was taking. Carter didn't refer to his dad in glowing terms. They seemed to share a distrust of the older man, but family was family and she still had a tangled past with Carter that made her wonder how far he'd come from the entitled boy who once caught her watching him work out in the gym at the estate and laughed at her interest.

Being near him now was such a risk. She'd tried to move on, not think of herself as the second-best Wilde sister, but memories of Carter and the attraction that still seemed to beat inside her had the power to flip her back to that insecure mental place.

She stared at the screen until the numbers blurred. Shifting and typing again, she started texting.

I agree to the terms we discussed. I stay in the cottage and you leave me alone.

She winced at the tense tone but hit Send anyway.

Carter shot back a text response almost immediately.

How could I say no to that charming agreement?

"They were your terms, but fine," she grumbled as she thought about what to write next. She couldn't exactly admit she thought his family had something to do with her dad's death. That would shut down all access, and this access onto the property only just opened for her thanks to Carter's offhand suggestion.

Before she could come up with the right response, another text popped up from Carter.

When are you coming so I can be ready?

She wished *she* could be ready.

Why, are you going to change the sheets for me?

She bit her lip as the Sent notification appeared on her screen. Then a wave of panic hit her. She didn't mean to sound flirty or interested or even happy about any of this…even though she kind of was. The whole trip over she thought about Carter and that sexy smile when she should have been thinking about her dad and Gena and how good it would feel to finally beat the Jamesons at their own game.

And bed? Why did she mention a bed?

I thought we established that I know how to clean. I actually have many skills.

She absolutely did not remember conceding that point. And the skills comment could not be flirting. If they started a game of mutual flirting her control would fizzle. But he had looked cute with that mop in his hands…

You used a mop without hurting yourself.
Congratulations.

I'm sighing at you right now.

She could almost hear him and the idea made her laugh. She smothered the sound as soon as it escaped her. But she didn't type fast enough. Another text flashed across her screen.

Trying again…when are you coming?

This time she switched to calling because, really, she wanted to hear his voice for this one. The element of surprise was on her side. She intended to enjoy that.

He picked up on the first ring. His deep, rich voice filled the line. "Hello, there."

The whole shivering in her stomach thing hit her again. It was unnecessary. She needed her reaction to Carter to stay…flat because she needed to keep her defenses strong against him and remember what happened to Gena when she didn't. She struggled to find that tone when she responded.

"I'm here now. Unlock the gate." When he gasped, she hung up.

This round to her.

Four

Carter refused to admit he jogged to the gate. It was a quick walk and he only picked up the speed to avoid being rude. He couldn't just leave Hanna hanging out front. He wasn't a complete jerk, after all.

As he walked down the long drive, he spotted her peeking between the bars of the electric front gate. She wore jeans and a purple Henley, both formfitting to the point where his brain power kept blinking out.

The temperature was cool but not cold like it had been at their last meeting in New York. A bag and what looked like a rolled-up jacket sat at her feet. That's all she had. A few things in an oversize duffel. Carter had no idea if that was a statement on how little she owned or on how short of a time she planned to stay. Either way, his brain had turned traitor on him because he was stupidly excited to see her. He could feel his mouth curl into a smile as his gaze wandered over her hair and that ponytail. The second he recognized the unwanted excitement racing through him, he tried to tamp it down.

At his worst in those days after his father kicked him out, he'd run into Gena and they spent a weekend together. It had been fun but meaningless for both of them. Flirty but nothing more.

He hadn't felt a shot to the gut when he saw Gena like he did when he saw Hanna again, which had a weird vibe both because they were sisters and because Gena was dead.

He smiled, trying to forget the twisted road that brought them to this place. "You're here."

She watched his hands as he punched in the code and the electric gate rumbled open. "You don't sound surprised."

"You have to admit I offered you a pretty good deal." He let the gate roll past him, then gestured for her to step inside. "Free housing and food with no expectations in return."

He felt the need to say that. To be clear he wasn't his father. He'd been trying to make that distinction with people his whole life.

"You're a prince."

"I'll take that as a thank-you." Because he was pretty sure that was as close as he'd ever get to gratitude.

"Should I be coming in this way?"

It had taken her less than ten minutes to lose him in conversation. "Huh?"

"I've always used the door on the side gate."

"The…" Right, the service entrance thing. His

father had always been very clear on separating *the help*—his words—from those the family invited for a visit. "You can use whatever entrance you want."

"That's an interesting change."

"Is it?"

She shook her head as she reached down and grabbed her bag and jacket. "Never mind."

Without saying a word, he took the bag out of her hand and balanced the strap on his shoulder. It didn't weigh much, which renewed his curiosity about what she'd packed. "I know it's strange to come back to a place you used to think of as home. It took my sister-in-law-to-be's high-risk pregnancy to lure me back to the area. Little else would have worked."

For a second Hanna didn't say anything. She gnawed on her bottom lip as she eyed her bag, but then she seemed to snap out of the haze surrounding her. "I read about that. Derrick's fiancée, right?"

Finally, a topic Carter could handle without trouble. He stepped back, closer to the house, and Hanna followed. He waited until she was out of striking range, then hit the button to close the gate behind her.

It rattled to a close as he guided them toward the main house. "Things have evened out a bit with her health but the pregnancy is still risky. Derrick is an embarrassing wreck. He's driving Ellie, that's his fiancée, and us, right to the edge. It's taking all I have not to order him to stay home from work, but Ellie would kill me because then she'd be stuck with him."

"I don't remember that much about Derrick. He seemed pretty disconnected from the house by the time I started visiting."

"He was mostly away at college by that point.

He's five years older than me." Carter was thirty and Hanna a year younger. Carter knew most of the basics about her because Jackson had included those in the file, including the truth about Gena's car accident. The police and medical examiner had termed it a suicide. Hanna never contested the finding, which made Carter think it must have been right. A finding that had crashed through him on a rush of guilt and sadness when he'd read it.

Carter needed to talk with Hanna about all of it, but he didn't want to scare her off. There were so many secrets hovering between them and as much as Carter pretended not to care about what his father did or said these days, that unopened envelope sat on his dresser, taunting him. While it was true he'd offered her the chance to come and fight whatever demons she had, he'd also wanted her to come for him. Bigger than that, he wanted her to confide in him. He wasn't sure why that suddenly mattered, but it did.

Something in her called out to him. She seemed lost and a bit broken. He understood exactly how that felt and wanted to help.

The curiosity about whatever secret bound her to his father also drove him. The need to know the answer grew each day. Nothing in the background search on her provided a hint, and Carter would never ask his father. Doing so might bring him back to Virginia, and he didn't want to deal with his father at all.

Gravel crunched under their feet as they walked. Without any warning, she stopped and stared at him. "I'm not staying in the main house."

He balanced his foot on the bottom step leading

up to the front porch that spanned the front of the house. "I remember, but—"

"No."

He blew out a long breath, trying not to let frustration overwhelm him. "Maybe you could let me finish a sentence."

She nodded. Almost looked like she smiled, too, but if she did it flashed then was gone just as quickly. "Fair enough."

"Until ten seconds ago I wasn't sure you were coming because, clearly, you are unfamiliar with how a phone works." When she started to interrupt, he held up a hand to stop her. "My point being, if I had known I would have had the cottage cleaned and aired out. Since your arrival is a surprise, and a welcome one so don't get all grumpy on me, I thought we could wait in the house while I have the place readied for you."

"First, I did call you."

She had to be kidding. "Ten minutes ago, from the front gate, but go on."

"Do you want me to text you a message right now?"

That tone. She was messing with him. No question.

"I can imagine what that message would say." But it was tempting to let her try. Everything she did and said intrigued him, made him want to know more.

That time she did smile. Even let it linger. "Second, I clean for a living. I can handle the cottage… I *want* to handle it."

Maybe it would make her feel closer to her father's memory, but the idea still struck him as wrong. He wasn't hiring her. He was trying to help her, though it was pretty clear she planned to fight him with every ounce of life inside her. "You're not here to work."

"I actually am."

Damn, she was exasperating and he kind of loved that about her. Not many people outside of his family challenged him. Most bought into the supposed power behind the Jameson name, which was why he sometimes used a fake last name. He wanted people to know him for him, and that included her. "I mean, for me. You don't work for me."

"You gave me the speech about how no one would bother me. I don't want people skulking around the cottage."

He wasn't the type to be knocked speechless but he didn't have a comeback for that one. "Skulking?"

She shrugged, looking disinterested...except for the way she twisted her coat in her hands. If she tightened that death grip even a fraction she'd likely rip the material. He found her reaction interesting. Here she was, all cool and annoyed on the surface. Underneath it looked like something very different was happening. Maybe it was the stress of being back or that stupid envelope. Part of him hoped she was fighting off the same attraction that threatened to overwhelm him.

She was a puzzle he wanted to solve. Hot with all those curves and those big eyes. Her looks caught his attention, but something about her made him want to dig deeper. She wasn't the little girl he'd once known. She'd grown up, gotten strong, acquired an attitude and that shyness, if it still existed, was firmly banked. The whole package worked for him. Which probably said something about him. Something not great about being attracted to a woman who looked at all times as if she were ready to punch him.

The argument in his head about having people who could clean for her died in his throat. "You win."

She smiled again. This one was big and sunny and for a few seconds she dropped the assessing I'm-watching-you stare she'd perfected. "I'm shocked you conceded so quickly."

That made two of them. "I'm not unreasonable."

"We'll see."

The way she pushed, her refusal to back down... so sexy. It was a shame so many secrets stood between them. So much history. "Then we should head to the cottage."

"I know where it is."

That stubbornness could also be annoying. He made a vow to remember that, to focus on how much she seemed to dislike him, even without knowing he slept with her dead sister.

"Right." He held up the key. "But I have this. I'll escort you, run through some of the cottage's issues, like a sticky window we'll get fixed as soon as possible."

"I think I can handle it."

He dropped his arm to his side. "Indulge me."

"I already am."

He'd stayed away for a full day.

Hanna was almost impressed by Carter's restraint. He'd left her to herself in the cottage the first night, even though she had the sense he wanted to stay and oversee everything she did.

But looking out the window now she saw him crossing the lawn, heading in her direction. Her reprieve had ended.

Not that the time alone had amounted to much. She'd been determined to search the place. It was a long shot, even though the cottage had sat unused after her father passed, but since she hadn't uncovered a new angle in the decade since his death, she didn't have anything to lose by being here.

But she'd been sidetracked yesterday when everything touched off a memory. The blue curtains Gena insisted they hang for privacy. The beige couch with the flat cushion on the left side because that's where her dad always sat. Then she'd found a stack of boxes in the hall closet filled with Dad's long-sleeve shirts and baseball hats. With photographs and cancelled checks.

At least looking through things helped her to not dwell on Carter. Getting sucked in by his charm felt like a betrayal to her mom and to her sister. The Jamesons had landed so many blows on her family and now here she was, watching Carter stalk across the lawn and not being able to look away. Those confident strides. The way his jeans sat low on his hips, highlighting his fit body. She never wanted anyone to be different from the perception she had in her head as much as she wanted that for Carter.

Hanna sighed when she heard the knock. Since Carter owned the property, it's not as if she had a choice about opening the door. "Hello."

"You haven't left the cottage since you walked in here yesterday morning." He held up a white bag and shook it. "So, I brought this." Then he held up a brown bag with the logo from a local grocery chain. "And this. Nothing much. Just the basics."

Her stomach growled in response. Food. Man, that sounded good and the fact he thought to do it set off a tingling in her stomach. She'd eaten two breakfast bars in twenty-four hours. She might be able to eat the bag at this point.

"The place was filthy. Not years-without-a-basic-cleaning dirty, but not good." It also qualified as a bit more than a cottage. It was an eight-hundred-square-foot house with an open kitchen and a family room, one big bedroom and a loft, where she used to sleep with her sister. Tiny compared to the main house but then so were some hotels.

His eyebrow lifted. "Whose fault is that?"

"Well, I haven't been here for about a decade, so not mine." She took the bag out of his hands, leaving him with the groceries. "What's in here?"

"Does this mean I can come in?"

"Kind of depends on your answer."

She saw him smile as he stepped inside and closed the door behind him. His face was turned away from her, but she picked up that sunny open charm that seemed innate to him.

"Chicken and a salad." He shrugged. "I don't know. Fruit?"

She closed the top of the bag and stared at him. "Are you asking me? Shouldn't you know?"

"I didn't make any of it."

He sounded horrified at the thought of cooking, which made her wonder exactly how he survived in California for all those months without his usual staff of helpers. "Who did?"

"Lynette."

The fact he thought that was a full response almost made her laugh. "Who is she?"

"She works at the house."

He seemed to be dancing around the answer and that made Hanna want to keep poking. "Was that so hard to admit?"

"Since you're judging everything I say? Yes."

She had to admit she was. Sure, he had all the trappings of a rich guy. When he was younger, he had played the wealthy-boy role pretty well. Then there was the issue of her sister and what happened between them and all the strong-arming by his father. But when she dealt with Carter one-on-one she didn't see any of that. He was charming. He didn't make demands or act like he was better than her. He'd picked up a mop and actually seemed to know how to use it.

But it all could be a carefully crafted act. His father excelled at games and forcing people to do what he wanted. It wasn't hard to believe Carter learned his skills at home. Still, a nagging voice in her brain kept saying that Carter was not his father.

Another day with him and she'd have a serious case of whiplash.

"That's likely fair." She nodded toward the kitchen. "Come on."

She dropped the bag on the counter and went in search of plates. It was a good thing a few of the hours she'd cleaned had been dedicated to the kitchen. Her plan for the afternoon was to figure out where to go grocery shopping. She'd do that after she saw what he'd brought with him and ate a bunch of chicken, because it sure smelled good.

She turned around with plates in hand and there he was, sitting on one of the bar stools at the counter. He wasn't waiting to be served. No, he had dived right into the bag and started unpacking. She liked a man who prioritized food over everything else. And she was sure there was something else. He seemed distracted, as if he wanted to talk with her.

No, thanks.

Verbally sparring with him, though invigorating, would bump her off track. She could not afford to spend the day thinking about him or that face or that sexy walk of his. She needed to settle in somewhere and restart, which was the plan even before she saw him again, but she had to try this first.

"I'm sorry." He mumbled the words as he placed a piece of chicken on each of their plates.

Her hand froze on the lid to what looked like homemade potato salad. "For?"

"Your sister."

Her whole body went numb. "What?"

"I know she…died."

Hanna couldn't say anything, couldn't even choke out a word. Her mouth had gone dry and the words refused to form in her brain.

She'd tried to push thoughts of Gena away because being here, on the property with him, trusting him at all, was a slam against Gena. It had been six months and Hanna no longer cried every day, but she thought about her sister all the time. Her pain. Her fear. How desperate she must have felt at the end. How lost.

And Carter had caused Gena's confusion. At least

some of it. So, to drop a stale apology at the table while munching on chicken struck her as an insult. One she couldn't process.

Maybe it was the silence or the suffocating tension that suddenly filled the room, but Carter looked up. "Hanna?"

"What exactly are you sorry for?" Her voice shook as she asked the question. That shaking was nothing compared to her muscles. They strained until she had to grab on to the edge of the counter to keep from falling down.

"The accident." He slowly lowered the piece of chicken to his plate. "I remember her from years ago and from…"

"When?"

His shoulders seemed to slump. "We saw each other more recently."

Saw each other. Heat raced through her body. The rage-filled-throw-things kind.

"That's a pretty neutral statement." She dropped the potato salad container on the counter with a thud. "You didn't come back from California after she died."

He'd committed so many sins when it came to Gena. There was so much fault and blame. Since the second she saw him, that reality did battle with the need he touched off in her. The same need she tried to stomp out but it refused to extinguish.

His eyes narrowed as he stared at her. "I didn't know she passed until just recently."

"I tried to contact you." And his father showed up instead. First, in writing. Then in person. Gena was barely in the ground before Eldrick demanded that

Carter's name not be associated with Gena's in any way. There was only one way Eldrick would know about Gena and Carter—Carter had told him. Only one reason for his visit—to fix Carter's mess.

"I didn't find out until after I came to your apartment in New York," Carter said.

She shook her head, trying to decipher what he was saying. Gena died months ago, not days ago.

There was only one explanation. He was playing some sort of game with her and it made her feel queasy and sad. "You should leave."

His eyes narrowed but he didn't hop off the bar stool. "What just happened?"

"Please, just go." Or she would. Maybe she shouldn't have tried this at all. The offer had sounded too good to be true, and clearly it was.

"You know this is my house, right?" The edge in his tone was there. As if he had a right to be ticked off. No way.

"Then I'll go." Because she couldn't sit there and try to rationalize away his lies. That sexy drawl of his, the self-assurance, even the subtle charm and little jokes…they had reeled her in. Made her lower her defenses but now reality came back and slapped her in the face.

He wasn't two different people, which meant the guy she'd spun teen dreams about in her head and whose voice echoed through her even now was the same guy standing in front of her, lying. This was her nightmare. He actually was just like his father.

She hadn't unpacked her duffel. It sat on the coffee table in the living area. She snagged the strap and threw it over her shoulder. Took a quick look around but, honestly, whatever she left here didn't matter. She never got attached to anything, which made it easy to walk away.

Turning around, she ran right into him. Her hand went to his chest to steady her balance. The firmness registered first. The hard muscles under her palm… Despite everything, how much she still ached to explore every inch of him. Then she dropped it, not wanting one extra second of contact with him.

"Hold on." He reached for her but stopped when she flinched. His hands went into the air as if he were surrendering. "Okay, I get it. You're upset, so I'll go."

She wrapped her fingers around the bag's strap. Tightened until her palms ached.

"We're going to talk about this." Backing away from her, he nodded as he headed toward the door. "You can't keep running me off."

She absolutely could. So much of her life had been swallowed up by the Jamesons. Her sister. Her father. Even her mother was collateral damage. She could not invite them into her life again. "I don't think you want to hear the truth."

He couldn't miss her message. It's not as if she was trying to be subtle.

A nerve ticked in his cheek as he stood there. It took another minute before his jaw unclenched and he blew out a long breath. "Fine, you want space, you got it."

She waved in the direction of the counter. "You can take the food."

But he was already headed for the door. "Keep it."

"I don't need your charity."

He stopped with his hand on the doorknob and turned back around to face her. "One of these days you're going to realize I'm not my father."

"Don't count on it."

Five

Carter tried to block out the memory of yesterday's lunch fiasco with Hanna. He worked in the library, went for a run, but none of it helped. His gaze kept wandering to the cottage. His thoughts centered on how her mood had flipped. She'd been guarded since he'd first knocked on her apartment door in New York, but yesterday had been different. She'd shut down and he still wasn't sure why.

He'd been raised to be quiet, seen and not heard. He'd learned to tiptoe through disappointment and difficult situations by using a mix of acting like he didn't care and humor. He kept most of his relationships pleasant but shallow. Shallow was safe.

All of that practice meant he could charm his way out of most situations. He'd smile and engage in unimportant chatter. His brothers joked that he was the perfect party host. He kept the conversation flowing. And for the first month after his dad kicked him out, he'd spent a lot of time partying. The alcohol flowed freely, which had allowed him to capitalize on the whole life-of-the-party thing, getting sucked in deeper and deeper.

He'd stopped cold turkey after he blacked out. It only took that one time, that complete loss of control, to scare him. He'd realized he preferred the warm heat of scotch rolling down his throat to being with people…to doing anything. The realization was enough to turn him around.

He refused to give his father the satisfaction of breaking him, so he'd stopped drinking. But he had the very real sense he'd been on the verge of a full-blown addiction that would have dropped him to his knees.

But all of that was his secret and in the past. He'd refused alcohol since he'd been back home, but neither of his brothers were big drinkers, so they didn't seem to notice. But now, looking around the small conference room table just outside Jackson's office, Carter was tempted to dive in and tell them everything.

His brothers and Jackson were in fine form, joking as they reviewed plans for some new commercial building project that would bring in millions of dollars. It sounded fine to him but wasn't really his expertise. Which was why it didn't make sense for them to have called him in from Virginia this morning. But he'd come willingly, relieved to be away from the temptation of Hanna and his plans to confront her.

The building talk died down and Derrick spun his

chair around at the head of the table so that he faced Carter head-on. "So…"

One of the walls was all glass and faced the hallway and the desks and offices beyond. Still, Carter suddenly felt trapped. Spence, Derrick and Jackson all stared at him. Tension pressed in on him and he didn't care for the suffocating sensation one bit.

He also knew he needed to stop whatever nonsense was headed his way before it could start. "No. To whatever you're going to say. The answer is no."

"It doesn't work that way." Derrick took a long sip of coffee, leaving a charged silence in his wake. "I'm oldest. I get to be bossiest."

Jackson nodded. "We should put that on your business cards."

Derrick kept his attention on Carter. "Where have you been hiding and why?"

Carter looked across the table at Spence, then to his right to Jackson. They all paid attention now. None of them looked at files or paperwork or reached for the fruit and bagels sitting in the middle of the table.

Carter sensed a setup and decided to play it off. "I drove in, then tried to steal Jackson's coffee—"

Jackson cleared his throat. "In related news, I'd like a lock on my office door."

"I'm surprised it took you this long to come up with that idea." Spence laughed as he swooped in for the bagel closest to him.

Derrick being Derrick, he did not get knocked off stride by the chaos swirling around him. He hopped right back into the conversation where he left off.

"Not this morning. I mean that you ran off to do Dad's dirty work and then—"

Spence made a strangled noise. "Please rephrase that."

"Then you came back to town and subsequently disappeared for a few days." Derrick leaned back in his big office chair as he continued to talk to Carter. "Now you're here, with that blank look on your face."

"Blank?" He did not need this today, not when he'd spent the entire morning trying to decipher Hanna and the mystery of the envelope and gauge how to read her fluctuating moods. But turning the conversation away from wherever Derrick was heading could only be a good thing. So, Carter grabbed a mug and then the coffee pot. Skipped the sugar and went for black. A shot of caffeine might do him some good. "Sounds to me like you're not getting enough sleep."

"Nice try, but you're wearing your I'm-trying-to-come-up-with-a-lie face." Spence laughed at his own joke as he turned to Jackson. "Carter has been using that ever since he could walk."

Jackson shook his head. "I forgot how fun it was to deal with all of you in the same room."

"Consider yourself an adopted Jameson," Spence said as he spun the plate in the middle of the table and grabbed the cream cheese.

Jackson caught the spinning tray before items started to fly off. "No, thanks."

Derrick exhaled louder than necessary. He also scowled and generally looked annoyed. He'd perfected that look. "Let's circle back to the original question." Derrick aimed all of his focus on Carter. "What's up with you?"

Admitting he had Hanna hidden at the Virginia estate would only invite questions. Sure, he could insist she deserved closure and they owed it to her after what happened to her father on their property. But the truth was his reasons for inviting her were far more complex and confusing. He did it for her, but he also did it because, after years away from her, he didn't want the time with her to end. He was the guy who moved on but when she tried to make him do that, to leave her house, all he wanted was to stay.

He didn't get it. He couldn't explain it. He really didn't even want to analyze his reaction to her all that closely.

He took his time twisting off the cap on the water bottle. "You guys were all busy with your women—"

Spence whistled. "I dare you to say it that way to them."

"He's stalling and saying provocative things in the hope of throwing us off track. He thinks it's charming or something." Derrick's gaze hadn't wavered. It stayed locked on Carter as the conversation swirled. "Which makes me wonder... Do you have a woman of your own you're hiding somewhere, like maybe in a big house in Virginia?"

Derrick made the comment just as Carter swallowed, or tried to. The water came rushing back up his throat and he started coughing.

Spence snorted. "Well, well."

"That's telling," Jackson said at the same time.

Then, for once, and not when Carter wanted them to, they all stopped talking. Their joint attention focused on him until he had to fight the urge to squirm. Calling up all of his life-of-the-party reserve, he aimed for calm and nonchalance. "I've been doing some work on the Virginia property."

Spence dropped his bagel without taking a bite. "I don't know how you can stand being there."

"Not all the memories are bad." Carter said that more as an automatic reaction than with genuine feeling. He'd programmed his brain to downplay the dysfunction. To ignore his playboy father, his dying mother, and every snide comment about being a failure and a disappointment.

His father had been harsh and cold. He'd thought nothing of throwing them to the ground or pitting brother against brother in both emotional warfare and actual physical fighting. Dear ol' Dad insisted that behavior made them strong. Made them ready to take over the business. The same business he nearly bankrupted with his questionable under-the-table deals and lying.

"You held your engagement party there. We can all agree that was nice," Carter said as the most obvious escape from the conversation popped into his head. He'd walked in on something interesting at the party, complete with Spence and Abby fidgeting and adjusting their clothes and looking as if they'd been caught if not in the act, then right after it. "Spence seemed to have enjoyed himself. Want to talk about that, Spence?"

Spence just smiled. "Not when we're still talking about you."

Well, damn. That didn't work.

"Look." Derrick set his mug down. "We just want to make sure you're okay. That you're not…"

Carter almost hated to ask but he had to know what thought or word had Derrick, his usually practical and reserved oldest brother, glancing around the room and avoiding eye contact. "What?"

Derrick grimaced. "Lonely."

"Do we really care about that?" Spence asked, the sarcasm obvious in his voice.

"You don't have to stay at the estate. You can live with me." Derrick shook his head. "Ellie is upset you're not at our place already."

Carter couldn't figure out if Derrick was using his fiancée as an excuse or not. But he did know the soon-to-be parents deserved some privacy. "Thanks, but now that Spence moved in with Abby, you should take a break from housing wayward brothers for a month or so."

Derrick pointed at his second-in-command and friend to all of them. "Then live with Jackson."

"Wait…what?"

Carter debated saying yes just to see Jackson sputter some more.

"Answer this question." The squeak from Derrick's chair echoed through the room as he sat forward and balanced his elbows on the edge of the table. "Are you thinking about leaving again?"

For a second, Carter's brain scrambled as he rushed to figure out what Derrick was talking about. Then he remembered the scene a year ago when Derrick begged him to stay and promised a united front against their father. Carter had kept on walking, a move he regretted because it sent a message to his brothers that he'd never meant to send.

This was a conversation they'd all avoided since he'd been back, as if by silent agreement. Carter didn't want to broach it now, but he didn't want Derrick to worry either. "Why would you think that?"

"You delivered the letter to Hanna Wilde as Dad insisted, right?" Derrick stared at Carter until he nodded. "That means there's nothing holding you here. I get that you want to move on, but I was hoping… I'd like you to stay. At least until the baby is born."

Derrick was one of the smartest, toughest people Carter knew and here he was, sounding like he was begging his baby brother to stick around for a few more months. Carter hated that his tendency to leave difficult situations—the family, any state where their father lived—meant Derrick felt he had to plead. He'd definitely screwed up with the way he'd handled leaving a year ago and this was the result.

"I'm not going anywhere." Carter pulled back from saying more before he made a promise he couldn't keep. "I mean, I know I'm not one to stick around, but as long as Dad isn't here, I'm here."

Jackson cleared his throat. "Is there anything else you want to talk about?"

The sentence was cryptic, but Carter understood Jackson was referencing Carter's ideas about the future of the estate. Now was not the time. Carter still wasn't sure those ideas were even the right ones for the business or for him. "No."

Spence looked at Jackson. "What's this about?"

Jackson looked at Carter an extra beat before turning back to Spence. "Nothing."

"So, you're hanging out in Virginia. You plan to stick around, at least for now." Derrick smiled as he spoke. "Got it. But what about the woman part?"

Carter should have seen that turn coming, but he didn't. It took his brain a second to unscramble. "We aren't talking about my love life."

"Actually, he was talking about fun. Some dating. A little sex." Spence pointed at Carter. "You're the one who mentioned love, which is not something any of us will forget."

"I'd like to," Jackson mumbled under his breath.

"And with that, I'll be heading back to Virginia." Carter stood up. He'd walk there if he had to, just to get out of this conversation.

"Hey." Derrick didn't raise his voice. If anything, he grew quieter. "Thanks."

"I'm here because I want to be here." Carter needed to make that point. His brothers could count on him even though he'd failed to show that to them in the past.

"Just let us know if that changes," Spence said.

"Done."

Carter didn't get very far before Jackson caught up with him. In silent agreement, they both stopped walking and stood in the busy hall with phones ringing at desks all around them and the low rumble of voices filtering through the melee.

"I'm trying to figure out how brothers who are so good at loyalty and business, despite their idiot father's meddling, can stink at interpersonal stuff." Jackson shook his head. "Your ideas for the property, Carter. That was a perfect opening to talk it over."

"Not yet." He still hadn't fulfilled his part of the agreement—a fact he knew because he still had that damn letter, but his brothers didn't know yet. And without the three of them completing all of Dad's tasks, their father wouldn't officially turn the business over. He still held controlling interest.

Since Carter had vowed not to get into business with his father, that meant waiting until Derrick was officially in charge before moving forward with anything involving the Virginia property.

Jackson shifted his weight to the side to let two women from accounting pass by them. "Because?"

"I'm not ready." He hated being unsure of his place in the family business, but that's where they were. Jackson's frown suggested he knew that. "And you can stop looking at me that way."

"Is it possible you don't want to talk about the proposal because if you do, and Derrick wants to pursue it, then you're stuck here?"

Maybe that was another part of it. Settling in, creating roots, being a part of something. Not having the freedom to pick up and run to California for a few months. A part of him wondered if he'd ever be able to make the commitment to stay and rebuild his life here.

Another part knew the answer was no, not with all the memories chasing him.

"Did you get a psychology degree while I was away for a year?"

Jackson snorted. "I need one to deal with your family."

That probably wasn't far from the truth. Their dad had hired Jackson a few years ago. At first, Derrick had been skeptical but it hadn't taken long for all of them to realize he was competent and not reporting back to Dad. Jackson moved from business associate to friend almost immediately. "You love us."

"Some of you…" Jackson smiled. "But only sometimes."

Six

Guilt gnawed at Hanna as she walked the fence line closest to the main house. The red and orange leaves blanketing the lawn provided a nice change of scenery compared to her morning of dismantling and searching the cottage.

If anyone had seen her through the cottage windows, they would have thought she was cleaning. But the real goal was to find her father's journal, hoping it would provide some insight into how and why he really died. But nothing so far, so she went out for some air.

She walked, letting the cool breeze catch the loose hem of her sweater and billow up inside. The lawn was awash in color as the trees dropped their leaves. The fresh air recharged her. She'd spent the hours, the whole night, really, since kicking Carter out of his own cottage trying to think of a better way to handle her unwanted feelings for him and how guilty she felt for having them.

Her father had died. Her sister had died. Gena's baby had never been born. With that much loss came a load of distrust. Hanna had aimed it all at Carter when his father was her true target.

Not that Carter remained blameless. He'd taken a back seat when it came to dealing with Gena and he'd let his father handle everything. That made him weak, not evil. Only, the pieces didn't fit together for her. The man who'd hunted her down didn't seem like the type to evade responsibility.

But her sister's warnings still rang in her ears.

Don't trust the Jamesons. Carter ran away. He will do anything to hide his mistakes.

She heard the crunch of dying leaves before she saw him. Looking up, she watched as Carter walked toward her with his hands stuffed in his pockets. One thought filtered through her memories: no one looked better in faded jeans and a plain black jacket than he did. From the broad shoulders to that trim waist to those long legs, he had the body of an athlete, which he had been at one time.

He stopped a few feet away from her as if he wasn't sure if he was welcome to come closer. "You're outside."

Words backed up in her throat. "Yes."

He blew out a long breath. "I see you're sticking with curt responses."

She hated that these feelings welled up inside her and spilled over. She wasn't this person. She didn't usually snap and act like a jerk. Life had taken an unexpected left turn on her, but she tried to stay positive. The only thing guaranteed to throw her off stride was the name Jameson.

The inner battle between wanting Carter to be the man he appeared to be and the memories of his father showing up unannounced, waving around Gena's bills from the health-care clinic, caused a mental clash. Bills he shouldn't have had. The same ones that referenced her pregnancy. Carter hadn't mentioned that part when he'd spoken of Gena. He'd acted as if he didn't know.

Why did she have to keep convincing herself that was just an act?

But there was one truth she could share without trouble. "About yesterday… Let's just say I'm protective when it comes to Gena."

"I have brothers. I get it." He nodded. "And I knew her, Hanna."

That did it. She could almost hear the door creak open. She debated rushing through it, peppering him with questions. Once she started, she knew she wouldn't stop, but maybe she could peek in. "How?"

He frowned. "What?"

"What was she to you?"

His shoulders stiffened along with his jaw. "The way you're asking makes me think you know."

"I want to hear your definition." She inhaled and walked through, even as dread settled over her, creeping in until she could barely hear. "Dating? Using her? Sleeping around?"

"Is this why you're ticked off at me?"

"Your family…" What did she even say next? She had no idea how to start a conversation that ended with *you ignited an emotional firestorm that swallowed my sister.* "Forget it. I'm here, at the estate, for one thing."

"Which is what exactly?"

Answers. Closure. Revenge.

"I thought you were going to give me space and not ask questions."

"Hey." He reached out and took a step toward her but stopped when she pivoted away from his hand. "Okay. No touching. I get it."

Something about the easy way he waded through this conversation set her off. This wasn't about her old crush or the attraction that kept sparking even though she would give anything for it not to. This was about the pain she'd tried to lock away and her imperfect sister, who deserved better. "You think you can just swoop in and take whatever you want. That people's feelings don't matter."

His head jerked back. "Where did that come from?"

"Gena was my sister. We talked about what was happening in our lives. About who was in them." The rest threatened to spill out of her. Every horrible fact.

"Wait a second." His hands were in the air and every movement seemed careful, as if he expected her to blow and he was trying to manage the situation. "Gena and I had a fling. A meaningless fling."

With that, Hanna's mind went blank. For a second she couldn't say anything. Her mouth dropped open and it took all of her strength to close it again. "You're such a man."

"Which I'm assuming is a really bad thing in this scenario." His hands dropped to his sides.

"It's not good."

A lawn mower started in the distance. The motor drowned out the sound of the gentle swish of the trees. Looking up at the house, she saw a woman open the balcony door on the second floor and then scurry back inside. It all felt so ordinary when this conversation was anything but.

"What do you think happened between me and Gena?" he asked.

If he wanted to do this, fine. She'd heard the story from Gena. Well, *a* story. Gena had a habit of embellishing, but she always started with a truth and that's the part Hanna couldn't forget. "You found her, took what you wanted and then blew her off."

"That's not true. Not any of it."

"Oh, please." The fact that he out-and-out lied crushed something inside her. She'd hoped he would... She didn't even know what.

He shook his head. "We had an agreement. We were clear—it was fun only."

Fun? He had to be kidding. "Do you know how she died?"

"Car accident."

That would have been terrible but the truth was so much worse. "She ran the car off a bridge. No brake marks. No other vehicles. It was on purpose. She was lost and alone and wanted to die."

All of the color drained from his face. "I'd heard the rumors, but are you sure?"

A new pang of guilt settled in her chest. Before Gena showed up at the door, Hanna hadn't seen her sister for a few months. "I was with her after you left. She came to me broken and distraught."

"Hanna, I'm not sure what you're thinking here, but your sister and I spent exactly one weekend together."

That couldn't be right. "No."

"Three days." He held up three fingers as if to emphasize his point. "That's it."

Gena's story unraveled in Hanna's head. She talked about Carter looking her up and all the dinners and gifts…then he was gone without warning. She'd talked in terms of months, not days. "That's not… You're downplaying the relationship to make yourself feel better about what happened to her."

"I can give you the exact dates if you need them, but that was it. This wasn't a big love affair for either of us." He never broke eye contact. Didn't fidget or stumble over his words. He spoke as if he believed what he was saying.

"She and I specifically talked about what you meant to her." It had killed Hanna. After all those years of admiring him from afar. All those computer searches she did as a grown-up just because she wanted to see what he looked like now.

"A weekend, Hanna."

The words refused to settle in Hanna's brain. His explanation didn't match anything she'd been told.

He took another step, closing the gap between them but not making any move to touch her this time. "Are you saying she drove the car off the bridge six months after our weekend together because of me?"

His voice shook. The stunned horror was right there on his face, in his words. He looked pale and unsure, his usual confidence gone. Nothing about his expression or the way he stood there fit with a man who didn't care that the mother of his child was dead.

She'd stoked her anger at him and painted him as one type of guy in her head because it was easier to heap the blame on him. She was self-aware enough to realize that. But only one person had been in the car that night. The police had been clear about that.

Gena had struggled her entire life with mood swings and those few months pushed her too far. Finding out she was pregnant, something she hadn't even realized until she felt sick, pushed her right to the edge. Carter's choices played a part in that, but only a part.

She couldn't blame him for Gena's choices no matter how much easier that would be. "No. That's not... I'm not arguing cause and effect."

"Then what are you saying, Hanna?"

Too much. Not enough. Tension gripped her until she thought she would shatter. He hadn't mentioned the baby or his father's insistence that every fact surrounding Gena's relationship with Carter be kept quiet, so she held back. Then there were all the other secrets about his family. So many things she suspected and now wasn't sure he knew.

She had no idea how or if she should spill it all. There just was no way for her to win. "Nothing. Forget it."

"How do you expect me to do that?"

"I'm sure you'll be fine." He would always be fine because he had the Jameson name to fall back on. That was the point.

She couldn't breathe. It was as if a tight fist had

closed around her chest. She fought off the need to gasp. The cottage. Quiet. She needed both.

She spun around, intending to go back to the cottage but she lost her balance. Carter's hand shot out. He caught her, then let go as soon as he steadied her.

He started talking as soon as they separated again. "Why do you think we were together longer than a few days?"

"You were bored. You, handsome and rich, this guy she knew as untouchable growing up, breezed into her life." That made sense to Hanna. It fit with his lifestyle and all that money. Everywhere she looked right now was a reminder of his great big piles of it. That, alone, should make her write him off but every time she tried she'd think up a new excuse for how his confusion might be real. "She really didn't stand a chance."

He zipped and unzipped his jacket. "She picked me up in a bar. Everything that happened was mutual."

"I didn't say it wasn't."

"I was a mess when I was with your sister. Not because of her. Because of everything else happening. I was wild and out of control, which she knew. Drinking too much and making bad choices. She said we could be wild together, then move on." A harsh sound escaped his throat. "Did she tell you that part?"

None of that fit. The drinking and bad choices sounded like Gena. She'd spun out of control after their dad died and never regained her balance. But the rest was so different from what Gena described. For a second Hanna wondered if her sister made up the relationship story because of her fears over being pregnant. She had been so shaky there at the end.

As soon as Hanna thought it, a new wave of guilt smacked into her. Was she just trying to think of ways to excuse Carter's behavior?

The lawn mower moved closer. The guy riding on it wore earphones. When he saw them, he did a double take. All it took was a raise of Carter's hand and a shake of his head to have the guy turning the machine around and heading off to mow another section of the land.

Carter waited until the noise quieted down and they were alone on that stretch of lawn to talk again. "I'd had a falling-out with my father. He kicked me out of the family, Hanna."

"But how serious could that have been? You were able to tap into your checking account to roam all over California. You're here now, so you're clearly welcome again." Because that story fit with how she needed to see him to keep some distance from him. If he'd really been pushed out then another piece of her defense against wanting to spend time with him would fall.

"Do you really want to talk about my finances?"

She didn't want to know anything. She didn't want to fight or to feel anything. All she needed was for him to see that what happened might not have been as simple as he thought. "You don't think, maybe, that you used her? That she was convenient and when she stopped being convenient, you left. After…however long."

Every one of his muscles visibly stiffened. "I told you how long. Three days."

"Right." She could not wrap her head around that or how broken her sister really must have been to make the relationship sound so much bigger than it was.

"We used each other."

"But she's the only one who's dead."

The words sat between them. They echoed in her head as tension wrapped around her and Carter. She couldn't draw in enough air, couldn't figure out how to call back her sharp response.

She hated who she was when she talked about Gena. Her death cast this harsh darkness over everything. Hanna thought she wanted to hurt Carter, to make him feel half of the pain that pulsed inside her, but looking at him now, seeing the shock and hurt in his eyes, she didn't feel one ounce of peace. Just dizzy and tired. If this is what revenge led to, she didn't want any part of it.

His chest rose and fell on heavy breaths. "If you're going to blame me for Gena's suicide, then have the guts to say it. Don't dance around the accusation."

She couldn't form the words. She wanted to blame him, but the pieces were all mixed up in her mind now. "There were…things that happened after. It wasn't just you. It was the aftermath."

His mouth dropped open. "I have no idea what that means."

Her mind went to the baby. For the first time, she saw the threats Carter's father made in a different light. She'd always assumed that he'd demanded she stay quiet because Carter wanted to hide from the truth. Now she wondered if Eldrick really wanted to hide the truth from Carter.

She had no idea what to do with that possibility or how to tell him such a crushing thing. "Do you know your father came to see her?"

Carter took a step back. Actually looked like he lost his balance and stumbled. "When?"

"After your supposed weekend together."

He made a grumbling sound. "Stop saying it that way."

"I didn't mean to… Once you were gone."

"Why?"

The confusion in his voice added to her own confusion. "I thought you sent him to find her. To fix your mess. Is that not true?"

"He kicked me out, Hanna. I didn't see or talk to my father until Derrick and Ellie's engagement party a few months ago. Even then, we spoke for less than fifteen minutes and there was nothing friendly about it." All of the confidence, those charming smiles and the carefree attitude he carried around had vanished. "And that was well after Gena's death."

"But he's your father. He still cleans up after you."

Carter's stunned expression morphed into something else. Frustration pulsed off him. "I'm a grown man. I don't need *Daddy* to fix anything for me. And, honestly, he's the last person I would ask for help."

That fit with how her father used to talk about Eldrick, but not with anything else. "You're saying you didn't send him to see Gena."

"Of course not." Carter sounded appalled at the idea. "For what?"

"I wasn't there."

She wished she had been. If she had stuck around and continued to live with her sister she would have seen the relationship between Gena and Carter and she would have been there when Carter's father came knocking and making threats. She'd lived through her own version of his intimidation when he tried to bribe her after Gena died, but she hadn't been alone and afraid. Hanna couldn't imagine how scary that must have been for her sister.

Carter crossed his arms over his chest. "But you know what he said to her."

"To stay away from you." It was a sanitized version but good enough.

"That doesn't make any sense. I was already in California. And I never told Dad that I spent a weekend with Gena."

"Because you were ashamed of it?"

"Because in addition to the fact my sex life is private, I go out of my way not to tell him anything." The longer Carter spoke, the more his voice rose.

Every possible comeback froze in her head. Every word he said changed every fact she thought she knew. The ground kept shifting under her until she didn't know what to believe or think. "Fine."

"Fine? You basically accused me of lying and, worse, of driving your sister to her death."

That's not... "I didn't."

"You think I'm some spoiled rich kid, running to Daddy."

She fought off a wince. "Look around you, Carter. Do you blame me? A house the size of an elementary school is standing behind you. The pool, the guesthouse. All these acres so close to Washington, D.C."

And the estate was only a small part of the Jameson empire. She'd read the business articles. They

owned commercial and residential buildings throughout the area and down as far as North Carolina. The
business. The other houses. That didn't even touch
the cars, the money, the stocks and whatever else
they had acquired.

He nodded. "For what you're suggesting? Yeah,
I do blame you."

"We knew each other as kids. Maybe we weren't
friends but I remember you from back then. You
didn't act ashamed of the money or the family name."
He'd been cocky and proud. The guy most likely to
do anything. He partied and brought girls home when
his father was away on business.

"Do you want to be judged by things you did years
ago?"

She hated that he made her sound unfair, made
her feel that way. "I guess that depends on if I have
anything to hide."

His shoulders fell as he let out a long exhale. "You
are dead wrong about me."

"Possibly." She stood there, trying to hold on to
her preconceived notions of who she thought he was,
but they no longer fit him as cleanly as she thought
they once did.

"I'm not sure what I did to *you* to invite your distrust or what my father was doing six months ago,
but I am sorry about Gena." Carter unwound his
arms and let them fall motionless to his sides. "I really am."

A lump formed in her throat. She couldn't swallow it or clear it away because she believed him. She
forced a word out over it. "Okay."

"That's all you're going to say to me?"

Her mind spun. She tried to think of what to say and explain how she'd viewed him through this specific lens because it was easier for her to tag him as spoiled than deal with the actual man. And now her defenses and biases were crashing at her feet and the vulnerability left her shaky and uncertain.

When she didn't say anything, he did a quick look around, then nodded. "Enjoy your walk."

Then he was gone.

She didn't see him the rest of the day but his words, that pained expression on his face, kept running through her mind. She'd accused him and then tried to ignore every response he offered. It had been the only way to hold on to that wall of anger she'd built. Letting that go meant leaving room for the pain and grief to sweep in.

It was easier to hate Carter and his father than to deal with her sister's death. She'd constructed this scenario where Carter refused to take responsibility, and that had started crumbling. But maybe she wanted it to crumble because then her attraction would make sense and be okay. The guilt would evaporate.

She could no longer tell the difference between how she wanted to see him and how she needed to see him for self-protection.

As she lay on the bedroom floor, sprawled on the fluffy carpet she'd just vacuumed for the third time, she had to admit she wasn't that great at responsibility either. She'd walked away from her sister when Gena refused to ease up on the partying. She'd seen Gena spinning out of control and tried to help, but then hadn't stuck around for the last round. And now her sister was dead.

An ache started low in her stomach, then it traveled. It seeped through her veins and landed in her chest. The weight had her rubbing the heel of her hand against her breastbone in the hope of wiping it out.

She took one last look under the bed, just to see if her father had hidden anything there. He had been the type to squirrel away money, in random coffee mugs, tucked in an envelope on the underside of his sock drawer, curled up in a small bag and rammed into an old boot at the bottom of his closet. She'd found all of those hiding places, but money was not her target.

Dad said his journal didn't have anything but everyday ramblings inside and that he only kept it to drive away the loneliness that settled in at night. But she still wanted to find it. It was a long shot, but if the journal still existed she wanted to read it. Just to see if there were any hints about a falling-out with Carter's father or problems at the house that could explain her father's sudden death.

That's why she was there, but Carter wouldn't leave her thoughts.

She needed him to be a jerk. That fit the story she had in her head. If he was a jerk, then she could roll her eyes over her stupid teen crush and move on. She could forget him and be satisfied that she'd ripped up the bribery check his father had offered in return for her never contacting Carter and never talking to him about the baby.

She could still hear the steady beat of Eldrick Jameson's words, how insistent he'd been back then.

In her mind she remembered it as fury about the baby and Carter's choices, which she assumed Eldrick thought were beneath his son. Now she wondered if that tone really signaled desperation over something bigger.

She glanced up at the ceiling and the dark beams that gave the cottage a cozy chalet feel. Her gaze followed the one in the middle, then moved to the next. The old wood had a certain charm. A bit ragged and…discolored. Not all of it. Just a swath at the far edge of one beam. A square facing away from the main part of the room, as if someone tried to patch it and used the wrong stain.

She sat up, squinting and moving her head as if either would give her a better angle. When those attempts didn't work, she got up. Climbed on the armrest of the couch and reached up, but her fingers only grazed the wood. She needed something higher. With a quick look around, she spied the bar stool. It would be wobbly and not smart, so of course she was going to use it as a makeshift ladder.

After a quick run to the kitchen to fetch the hammer, she grabbed the bar stool. She didn't know if either item would help, but the off-color piece of beam would bug her all night if she didn't get a closer look.

As predicted, the bar stool shimmied when she put one foot on it. Balancing a hand on a couch armrest, she tried to find her equilibrium, silently cursing herself for not paying more attention to all that "core" talk in the free Pilates class she'd attended. After a few more seconds, she let go and stood up. One hand grabbed the beam, anchoring her a bit.

She ran her fingers over the scarred wood and

felt a ridge. With a tug, she pulled open a door she didn't even know was there and felt around inside what she now assumed was some sort of lockbox without any lock. A small metal box came out in her hand. Lowering it as she stepped off the stool, she peeked inside and shuffled through the contents. A folded-up birth certificate—her father's—and a passport, which had expired more than a decade ago. Two coins she couldn't identify and a photo of her parents.

They were young and smiling, so different from how she remembered them. They weren't the joking-around type. Mostly, she remembered the fighting and all those debates about visitation days and who got the kids for Thanksgiving each year. But looking now she could almost hear her father's deep laugh as she brushed her fingertip over the photo of his face.

She hadn't known she wanted to find something like this until she held it in her hand. Memories flooded her. Grilling hamburgers with him outside this cottage. They'd had to stay close to the house and not make too much noise or Dad's boss, Carter's father, would get angry. It was like this undercover game that ended with food and laughter.

She smiled as she reached for the last item in the box. A small journal, maybe six inches long, rolled up and secured with a rubber band.

Finally.

Seven

"You're smart to be inside," Jackson said as he walked into the Virginia estate's library. He shook his head and beads of water splashed to the floor. More ran off his raincoat. He shifted his weight as he looked down. "Crap. I didn't realize—"

"It's fine." Carter sat up and his back muscles groaned in relief. He glanced at the clock and realized he'd been sitting there for three hours without moving.

He blamed Hanna. He could not get her out of his head. Her face, that wary expression, the mix of pain and fire in her eyes as she talked about Gena. He didn't understand the accusations or how she came to her conclusions. He had no idea how she could stand to be in the same room with him believing what she did.

But her doubts fueled him. Ever since their rough conversation yesterday afternoon, he'd been on a quest to piece together his schedule and show Hanna how short a time he'd been around and with her sister.

It was a ridiculous task. Totally unnecessary. He was a grown man and his sex life wasn't Hanna Wilde's business. But the idea of Gena committing suicide made him sick. The thought that he might have done something or said something to push her there left him feeling raw and hollow. She was funny and irreverent and the idea of her taking her own life left him feeling numb.

He hadn't lied to Hanna. He and Gena had been nothing more than a quick hookup. When Hanna had suggested otherwise, he'd been desperate to clear his name. Still was. It was as if he needed her to believe in him. He hated the idea that he'd spent most of his time since seeing her again wanting to kiss her, touch her, all while she viewed him as an ass.

Jackson dumped his raincoat over the back of a chair and ran a hand through his hair. He nodded in the direction of the wall of files, papers and books stacked around Carter like a fort. "What exactly are you doing?"

"Working."

Bookshelves filled with everything from nonfiction to thrillers lined the room. The desk sat away from the wall by the windows. The dark wood club-like room sat on the second floor with a shaded patio just outside the double French doors.

Jackson dropped into the chair across the desk from Carter. "I thought you didn't work for your family."

Carter silently cursed Jackson's poor timing in

showing up for a visit now. "There are other jobs, you know."

"Uh-huh." Jackson tapped his fingers on the chair's armrest. "But you don't have one of those either."

"True."

The fragile wooden chair creaked as Jackson leaned forward and picked a piece of paper off the stack closest to him. He frowned as he scanned it. "Your credit card bill?"

Carter reached out and grabbed it. "When did you get so nosy?"

"Since I volunteered to come out here and see what you're really doing, I can't deny the claim." Jackson leaned back again, setting off a new round of creaking as the chair strained under his weight. "I'm here to poke around."

"My brothers sent you?" That should have been obvious from the beginning. They'd both texted earlier. Now he knew they were checking to make sure he'd be there when Jackson arrived.

"You know what *volunteered* means. We were sitting around, talking about how weird and secretive you've gotten. Then we drew cards to see who got to come out here and bug you."

The explanation sounded so odd that Carter knew it was true. "And you lost."

Jackson snorted. "I won."

Footsteps sounded in the hall. The person coming to visit was not trying to hide the entrance. Hanna stepped into the doorway perfectly dry but without an umbrella or raincoat. Carter guessed she'd dropped them downstairs, which left the question of how she knew where to find him.

"Lynette said I could come up." Hanna's steps faltered as her gaze landed on Jackson's back. "Oh, man. I'm sorry."

Jackson turned around as the chair tilted slightly to one side. "I'm not."

Hanna winced as she started to back out of the room again. "I had no idea you had company."

"It's fine." Carter watched her, looking for signs that she wanted to pick up where they left off yesterday. Her unreadable expression didn't give anything away. "He's more like family than company."

"Please stop saying that." Jackson got up and in a few steps stood in front of Hanna with his hand out. "Jackson Richards."

Her hand froze in the middle of lifting it. "Jackson?"

"You don't like the name?" Jackson glanced over his shoulder at Carter. "Or have you been talking about me?"

"Not really." But Carter had to admit the reaction was bizarre. She'd stopped moving and seemed to be stuck in some sort of haze. She looked at Jackson, her gaze searching his face as she frowned. "Hanna?"

That snapped her out of whatever emotion had her in its grip. She cleared her throat as she started shuffling again. "I'm sorry. I can come back."

The confusion and uncertainty surprised Carter. All of yesterday's anger had vanished but she came off as shaky and unsure. He didn't know what that meant, but he cared. Of course he did. He couldn't seem to stop caring about what she was thinking and feeling.

"From where?" Jackson asked.

She slammed to a halt. "What?"

"You're already on the grounds and in the house. That's not an easy feat, by the way. That gate out there is no joke. I have a key and a security code and you move around easier than I do." Jackson kept his voice low and soothing. The tone carried a hint of welcome and amusement. "My point is that it seems easy for you to get in and out, which I assume means you're staying nearby. Possibly *very* nearby."

Carter wanted her closer. In the house, with him, touching him. Needs he'd hidden as he tried to figure her out. "Um…"

"It's not…" She bit her lower lip. "Yeah."

Her voice, that stumble. Suddenly, Carter didn't feel so alone in the battle with his attraction for her. They had so much to talk about and think through, but all of that fell away as he watched the slight blush cover her cheeks. Maybe what they both needed had nothing to do with the past and other people.

Jackson looked back and forth between Carter and Hanna. "For the record, you two are not good at this."

"What?" she asked.

Jackson waved a hand in front of him. "Whatever this is."

Silence filled the room. Hanna did a lot of staring—at Jackson, at the hardwood floor and the expensive Oriental rug covering it, at the antique cherry desk Carter sat behind, at the bookshelf on the opposite wall. Finally, she focused on Carter. "Do you trust him?"

Carter appreciated the easy question because everything else between them had gotten so complex. "Completely."

Jackson let out a long, labored breath. "I can hardly wait to hear what comes next."

"I'm Hanna Wilde." She stepped fully into the room and this time shook Jackson's hand.

Now it was Jackson's turn to freeze. It only lasted a second. Carter doubted Hanna even noticed. But Jackson wasn't one to get knocked off stride and that extra beat of hesitation meant he wasn't expecting to hear that name.

Carter couldn't help but smile at the idea of Hanna getting the upper hand on Jackson.

"Oh, you're the one..." Jackson nodded. "Yes, hello."

She glanced at Carter and he didn't even try to hide the fact that her name would have clued him in. "He knows my father wanted me to find you."

Carter expected anger or frustration, maybe some yelling. Instead, she let out what sounded like a resigned sigh before turning back to Jackson.

"Then I can shortcut this." She stepped closer to the desk. "Carter's dad wanted me to have this envelope, but I don't want anything to do with the man or his games. Since my father used to live and work here, Carter offered that I come back to say a final goodbye and collect some of his things. I thought maybe I could also figure out what Eldrick wants without ever having to deal with him again."

Jackson's eye widened. "You said it all in one breath."

"That was impressive." And Carter meant that.

"Especially since I didn't expect to say it at all."

Hanna walked over to the chair Jackson had abandoned and sat down. "Me being here is a secret."

"Okay, I'll play along. From whom?" Jackson asked.

She shrugged. "You, I guess. And Carter's brothers."

"I'm lost," Jackson said as he leaned against the bookcase next to Hanna's chair.

Carter empathized. "It's your turn. I've been in that state since I tracked her down."

She frowned at him. "Like your mental state is my fault."

Lately it was. Being this close to her, even with Jackson there, sent a spike of energy buzzing through the room. "Well…"

"Okay, let's go back to the Eldrick part." Carter braced his hands on the bookshelf behind him. "You don't know what he wants?"

She shook her head. "No."

Jackson looked from Hanna to Carter and back again. "Here's a suggestion, and I admit this may lack finesse, but why don't you just *open the envelope*?"

"She doesn't want to be manipulated." Carter understood that much.

"The Eldrick piece is only part of it. I also wanted to take care of my dad's belongings, the stuff Eldrick never turned over."

Jackson looked more confused, not less. "It's like you two are talking in code."

"Bottom line?" Hanna shifted until she faced Jackson. "I don't trust Carter's father."

Carter understood that. It was the part where she didn't trust him either that kicked him in the gut. He sat there wanting her, spent the night dreaming about her, and he'd bet she could walk away from him and not look back. He hated that. Hated that she refused to confide in him. But he really hated that he cared this much.

"You're smart to stay away from Eldrick. The guy has a tendency to destroy the people he touches," Jackson said.

Her eyebrow lifted. "Don't you work for him?"

Jackson made a humming sound, the same noise he tended to make as he thought through what he wanted to say. "I prefer to think that I work for Derrick."

Hanna glanced at Carter. "Does he?"

"Yes. We're hoping that soon Dad will fully retire, hand over the reins and everyone will work for Derrick."

Carter vowed to do whatever he had to do to make that happen. Unfortunately, the very stubborn, very hot and utterly compelling woman sitting in front of him played a part in that. She hadn't opened the envelope yet, but he was betting that she would soon. That curiosity would win out.

"Except you, of course." Jackson mumbled the comment but he got everyone's attention.

She asked, "Wait, you mean Carter really doesn't work for the family?"

"Technically, he doesn't right now." Jackson smiled.

Their back-and-forth about him without talking to him was more than a little annoying. "*He* is sitting right here."

"Well, my response is the same." Jackson shrugged. "I get not wanting to be manipulated by Eldrick but every day the envelope sits there you have to think about him."

She didn't even hesitate. "I made a vow months ago. No more letters from Eldrick."

"Then I'm out of options." Jackson pushed away from the bookcase and straightened. "Which means it's time for me to go."

Carter decided to interpret the remark for her just in case she didn't get it. "He plans to run back to my brothers and report that you're here."

Jackson walked over to his soggy coat, picked it up and slipped it on. "He's right."

The chair practically bounced against the floor as she stood up. "You can't."

"Because?" Jackson stopped buttoning the raincoat and waited a few seconds as he shot her a *well?* look. "See, if you can't answer that question, then I don't understand the need to keep the secret."

"I don't want Eldrick to know I'm here." Her voice vibrated as she spoke.

Carter got it and took pity on her. "Then you're safe."

"The one thing you'll figure out about the Jameson brothers, if you don't already know it—they stick together." When she started to talk, Jackson talked louder and finished. "And the thing they're the best at doing is creating a united front against their father."

She didn't say anything. Just stared at him. Carter waited for a sharp response but she looked lost in thought, not angry. All signs of yesterday's frustration had disappeared. He wasn't sure what that meant but it gave him hope.

"I'll be off." Jackson waved to Carter before smiling at Hanna. "Nice to meet you. We'll see each other soon."

Her mouth opened and closed a few times before she spoke. "Will we?"

He winked at her as he walked out of the room and disappeared into the hallway. "I can almost guarantee it."

Once they were alone again, Hanna turned back to Carter. "I didn't mean to—"

"Here."

Carter didn't know if Jackson still hovered in the hall and he didn't care. This topic was too important. It had consumed his entire morning because he needed her to believe in him.

She shuffled the paperwork in her hands, paging through it but not spending much time on any one piece. "What am I looking at?"

"Proof. It represents my whereabouts around the time I saw your sister again. My calendar. Some receipts that show where I was and when." He'd collected and printed off all of it before Jackson came in.

She dropped her hands to her lap. The papers hung loose in her fingers as she stared at him.

He had no idea what that meant, so he kept pushing his case. "I was outside Charlottesville, where your sister lived, for what looks like seven days because I'm missing some verification, but the real answer is three." He pointed at the receipts resting on her knee. "You can see the plane ticket and the hotel receipts."

She looked at him for a few more seconds then glanced down. "You stayed in dive motels."

"What?"

She shook her head. "Nothing."

"The point is, this big love affair or whatever you think happened between me and Gena isn't real." The driving need for Hanna to see him as decent pushed him. "I can't provide proof that we agreed to hang out for a few days before I left for California because those were discussions without witnesses, but I can give you all of *that.*"

She balanced the papers on the edge of the desk. Didn't rifle through them or demand more verification.

"Why did you do this?" Her voice stayed soft. No judgment or anger.

He could ignore the question or come up with some flippant answer. That's how he usually operated. Kept things shallow. But he needed her to know the truth.

"Because, believe it or not, I care what you think about me." His hand cramped. When he looked down he realized he had a death grip on the armrest of his desk chair. Easing up, he unwrapped his fingers and let the circulation return to his hand.

"Why?"

He rubbed his right palm. "I wish I knew."

Hanna visibly inhaled then exhaled. It was as if she were trying to slow her breathing. "She told me... She said you two were..."

Since he dreaded what word she might come up with he used one of his own. "Dating?"

"Something like that."

"It was nothing like that." Not even close. He enjoyed talking with Gena but a few hours of that gave way to something else. She moved in a way that was almost erratic. She'd start a conversation, then break it off and start talking about something else. The sentence fragments never connected. She operated in chaos. "Look, I don't want to tick you off again, but I do have to say your sister was struggling."

"Struggling how?"

"Operating without boundaries. Nothing seemed to be off-limits." When he realized he was fidgeting, he folded his hands together on top of the desk. "I was drinking heavily back then and felt the full impact the next morning. She could outdrink me. She would wake up, ready for the next party."

"She'd never been great with rules but she kind of lost her footing after Dad died." Hanna's voice went from eager to listen to sad, sort of resigned. It was as if it were painful for her to say the words.

"I can understand that."

"You can?" She didn't sound skeptical. The tone was more like one of genuine interest.

The tension running through him eased. The sense of being on the edge of saying the wrong thing subsided. He hated this subject and never talked about it, but he felt like he owed it to her to explain. "After losing my mom I got hit with this mix of grief and how-could-you-leave-me-here-with-Dad anger and I really didn't know what to do with it all. My brothers were in college and I hated everything."

He wondered if Hanna's reactions now were due to grief, as well. Cancer and suicide weren't the same but the end result—standing on the sidelines while a loved one died—led to the same grief-soaked place.

"If you think I'm difficult to deal with now, you

should have seen how I acted in private back then."
She would have hated him. No question.

"You're not, you know."

She completed one of those conversational left turns that put him a few steps behind. "Not what?"

"You're not *that* difficult." It looked as if she were trying to hide a smile but the amusement in her voice gave her away.

The rest of the weight pressing down on him vanished. They hadn't settled much but he felt as if they'd reached some sort of common ground. That his worries about her viewing him as a useless playboy jerk might not be true.

He decided to test that theory. "Ever since we saw each other again you've been—"

"Dealing with your family is difficult."

Carter continued to rub his palm even though the slicing pain was long gone. "I'm not my father, Hanna."

"I know."

He blew out a rough breath. "That might be the nicest thing anyone has ever said to me."

"He wouldn't spend hours or days or whatever you did, tracking down evidence to get me to trust him." She picked up the top piece of paper, then put it down again. "That's something."

Probably too much. Vast overkill and a statement on his difficulties with dealing with people on more than a superficial level. But he wanted deeper with her. He had no idea why, but he did. "It sounds like you might actually like me."

She laughed as she held up a hand. "Let's not get carried away."

In that moment she sounded so free. The light tone sent a shot of need spiraling through him. But wanting her when there was still so much unsaid between them struck him as dangerous. "Is there anything I can do to help with your quest?"

"That's an interesting word."

If he knew what she was looking for or what she wanted to prove or avoid he would have chosen his words more carefully. As it was he only knew *something* was up. He was not the guy people went to for help, but maybe he could give her this before they both moved on, because that was inevitable. "If you find something negative about my father, something you need help with, let me know. We'll take care of it."

"What about family loyalty?"

He couldn't blame her for asking. "That only extends to my brothers, Jackson and a few others."

"Really?"

When she'd asked a question like that a few days ago, even yesterday, it came with a slap of disbelief. He'd seen it in her eyes and heard it in her voice. But this time it sounded like she wanted confirmation. That he could do it. "Do you know how Derrick ended up at the head of the company?"

She shrugged. "I figured it was a birthright thing."

He was pretty sure that was a knock on the size of his bank account, but he let it go because they were finally talking. He rarely had a chance to reason through these things with anyone. Letting outsiders into his family dynamic wasn't an option when you were a part of a family that landed in the news too often.

"He saved the company from my father's misman-agement and questionable deals. Dad doesn't really have the ability to distinguish right from wrong." Which Carter was pretty sure qualified as the big-gest understatement he'd ever uttered. "I can give you the details if you want them. Suffice to say, Derrick was ready to go public and burn it all down. Spence and I supported him."

"But you would have lost everything."

He got the sense that the state of her bank ac-count didn't matter much to her except to know she could take care of herself. But her obsession with *his* money, in terms of believing that it somehow defined him, was a huge frustration for him.

"Not everything, but a lot. But stuff doesn't matter all that much in the face of right and wrong."

She shot him an are-you-serious glance. "You do know you're a Jameson, right?"

"I'm reminded quite often." By the gossip press. By people at the office. By the estate and now by her.

"Including by me."

At least she didn't deny it. He decided to consider that progress.

"So far, yes. I'm hoping to change that. When you look at me I'd like for you to see me and not my fa-ther." He didn't mean to say the words but he'd never been more serious in his life.

"Lunch would help."

The turn of topic had his brain misfiring for a second. Then he focused on the lilt in her voice and the half smile she'd worn throughout most of their conversation. Something had happened to change her mood. His had changed, as well. The question was if they could sustain it or if they'd slip back into arguing mode.

"Why, Ms. Wilde. Are you using me for my access to food?"

"I bet there's a really big kitchen in this house." She stood up and glanced at him with one eyebrow raised, as if in challenge.

"Wanna see my pots and pans?"

She shook her head. "That's a terrible line."

"I have others." This time when he turned on the charm he intended to show her who he really was. He was not that shallow guy and he was tired of having people think he was. "Come downstairs with me and I'll let you hear some."

He got up and came around the side of the desk until he stood in front of her. "Your lines keep getting better."

He guided her toward the door, ignoring the buzz that moved through him when he put his hand on her lower back. "You are not going to believe how charming I am."

"Impress me."

He intended to do just that.

Eight

For the next several days Carter mostly left her alone, except at mealtimes. He'd show up with food or text her and joke about luring her to the main house with roasted chicken or something equally delicious.

Lynette prepared most of the food. Hanna had met her when she had ventured over to the house and accidentally met Jackson, as well. Lynette was a woman in her sixties with a touch of a German accent. She sang Carter's praises and grew quiet at the mention of his father. Hanna loved her priorities.

Jackson provided a different challenge. He had been charming and clearly close to Carter, despite the sarcastic comments. But meeting him made her uncomfortable, thanks to her father's journal. Most of the entries centered on her father's workdays and the television programs he liked and didn't like. But every now and then there would be a more personal entry. Sometimes about Eldrick's secrets. The man's sins worried her father. She didn't know if the cryptic "Jack" references in the journal were actually about Jackson, but she felt compelled to find out... somehow.

But not now. No, tonight she intended to concentrate on Carter. He'd brought pot roast to her cottage on this cool night. It was steaming and savory and she might need to run around the estate's many acres to work off enough to be able to sleep.

She dumped the dirty dishes on the counter next to the sink and leaned against it to watch him. "I'm starting to think you really do plan on wooing me with food."

Carter shot her a sexy smile as he continued to wash the serving plate. "Of course not...unless it's working."

"My pants no longer fit."

He chuckled as he dried the dish, then his hands and turned to face her. "Is that code for something?"

"Yeah, the fact I can't get the zipper up."

He wiggled his eyebrows. "Sexy."

Exactly, and that was a bit of a problem for her. Him cleaning. Him bringing her food. Him not assuming he could barge in and always asking permission first. Now that was sexy. The charm combined with that face and those sleek muscles were a sucker punch to her control. The more time she spent with him, the more her anger fizzled out. And she wasn't sure she was ready to let it go. Not after she'd been so wrapped up and furious for months.

During the day she'd think about him. Memories of that sly smile and deep voice would pop into her head and she'd forget why she disliked him. Those old feelings from childhood of being dazzled by him and blinded to his faults would rise up. She had to work to remember he was the same man who hurt her sister...though that was no longer as clear as it once had been.

Even she couldn't deny that her sister had embellished her time with Carter. She'd turned the reality of three or so days into what sounded like long-term dating. Now Hanna wasn't sure what she thought or what any of it meant, so she held on to what she did know—Carter's father had tried to blackmail her to stay away from Carter. He wasn't his father, but it wasn't that easy to separate the two.

Carter hung the now damp towel on the handle to the stove. "Did you want wine or anything?"

"I got the impression you didn't drink anymore, or maybe you still do and I don't—"

"Hanna?" With a palm resting on the counter, he leaned in until his mouth hovered just above hers. "You're on the verge of babbling."

"I'm trying not to be a jerk." For some reason the comment came out as a breathy whisper.

"If that happens, I'll let you know." His gaze wandered over her face like a gentle caress. It landed on her mouth and stayed there for a few seconds until he blinked and stepped back again. "But no, I'm not drinking. I figured out I value control too much. Also, it's too easy for me to lean on it."

"That's honest." She couldn't imagine the younger version of Carter ever admitting to having a problem.

All those magazine articles and gossip columns about the brothers and what a catch the bachelors were never mentioned anything except their strengths.

There had been references to their athletic promise and college years, but now that she thought about it, she couldn't remember ever reading a quote by any of the brothers themselves in all those posts. It was all photographs of them dating this woman or that one. About charity events and movie premieres. Nothing about who they really were, nothing like the real-life glimpse she'd been getting since she'd agreed to come to Virginia with Carter.

"I really don't want to test my ability to form an addiction." Carter moved around the kitchen, stacking and restacking dishes and cleaning the counters for a second time.

She knew nervous energy when it smacked into her, and that was exactly what was happening right now. "Did someone help you with that?"

His head shot up. "Like who?"

"A therapist? I think most people can't see they have a problem without assistance."

"If it had gotten worse, I'd like to think I would have gone to meetings or gotten help." He rehung the kitchen towel on the bar. "I know who I am without alcohol. I sort of fear who I am with it."

He created the opening, so she walked right through. "So tell me who you are, Carter Jameson."

She leaned back against the counter and sized him up. The conclusion was clear: a pretty outward package and a seemingly decent internal one. But she wanted to be sure.

"Irresistible, right?" he asked.

She didn't bother to lie. "A little."

That got his attention because he stopped fidgeting. "Oh, really?"

"You can't be immune to the impact of your charm." And he had to own a mirror. She refused to believe beautiful people couldn't tell they looked different from most people.

She could look in the mirror and see someone imperfect but pretty. She wore a solid size twelve, not tiny like her sister. Not someone who could walk around without a bra and be comfortable. A woman locked in a constant battle to keep a sliver of space between her upper thighs for comfort's sake.

Society might judge her as chubby but she saw a healthy person in the mirror. She loved food, which she balanced with walking and other exercise. Her whole life was about stability, about trying to maintain a middle ground. But Carter kept her totally off balance. The way his appreciative gaze swept over her made her feel beautiful, stunning and powerful.

"You know what I mean." She continued because he was staring at her right now with this silly, tempting grin. "You go through life looking like that, with money and resources and that voice. I'm betting women line up to meet you."

He balanced his hands on the counter on either side of his hips, mimicking her stance while standing across from her. "What if I told you a secret?"

Her heart rate kicked up. She could feel the blood race through her. "Do it."

"The charm, the whole guy-who-can-run-a-party thing, is an act."

Not what she expected. No, this was far more interesting than any tidbit of family or dating gossip. "You're faking it?"

"Not with you. I mean, it's not real out there." He nodded toward the window and the dark night beyond. "That's how I found my place in the family. Derrick is practical and grumpy, or he was until Ellie. Spencer is really smart and can always find the right angle to make something work. Me, I'm the one who entertains people. I put on an act so people can't see that I lack my brothers' talents. That, except for them, I don't like being a Jameson very much."

She searched her memories, all those informal football games the brothers played on the lawn and how they stopped to talk with her father, and she could see it. Carter kept things light. He beamed in like sunshine. To know that it was a facade, some act he created to survive in his family made her stomach churn. "I can't figure out if that's sweet or sad."

He shrugged. "Maybe a bit of both. Don't get me wrong. I know how lucky I am with the money part. Even after being cut off financially by my father, I had an account from my mom. Derrick insisted on paying me a salary. He still dumps money into it. I just ignore it because I'm fortunate enough to be able to. I don't have to worry about food or housing because my name is on the trust that owns this house, again thanks to my mom."

His body language said "no big deal" but something dark and clouded moved through his eyes. She noticed the dimming, the blink of pain, before he talked with that light tone.

"So, you turn on this charm offensive to get through events and—"

"Life."

A peek behind the curtain. That's what this felt like. A brief glimpse into the real Carter Jameson, though he made it sound like the real version was buried pretty deep. "You seem pretty genuine right now."

"I am. With you. I can't explain why, so don't ask." He pushed away from the counter and walked the few steps to stand in front of her. "Maybe it's because when I first saw you again I thought we were both a little lost. I viewed you as a kindred spirit. Or I did, until you kept kicking me out and walking away."

Yes. He got it. Behind the stability and the attempts to maintain equilibrium lurked a certain insecurity and a fear that running up against another Jameson would only make her life worse. "Sorry about that."

"It's good for me to have to work for it." He didn't touch her but he moved until he stood between her outstretched legs.

"You should keep working at it." This close, her breath caught in her throat. She felt it hitch. Felt her pulse thump in her ears until it sounded like banging.

He nodded. "I plan to."

Risking everything, forgetting the cons and the past, she lifted her hand and rested it on his chest. The heat from his skin seeped through his shirt into her palm. The touch reassured her, and when he covered her hand with his she felt grounded for the first time in a long time.

"The lost thing? I never thought of it that way, but it's probably true. I've spent my life being the dutiful daughter, the supportive sister, the one everyone could count on. With my whole family being gone, I'm not clear on what my role is anymore." She had to force every single word out, push them past this hard lump in her throat. She expected to get pummeled with a load of new guilt for having said what she actually felt. Instead, a weight she didn't even know sat on her chest eased. Not completely, but a bit.

His fingers threaded through hers. "You could try living for you."

"I wish it were that easy."

What she really wished was that he'd kiss her. Just swoop in and take away the doubts and give her a few minutes without thinking.

As if he could hear her thoughts, he leaned in until his mouth hovered right over hers. "Yes?"

She nodded as she shifted to meet him. "Please."

His mouth swept over hers, soft at first, almost searching. Then he lifted his head and stared down at her again. Whatever he saw there must have erased any concern, and it should have because she was all-in on the kissing. When his lips covered hers again there was nothing slow and gentle about it. His mouth captured hers in a scorching kiss. The world fell away. It was just her and him and the heat and the feel of his arms around her and his hands on her back.

He kissed her like he'd never see her again. The intensity of it shook her. Her skin felt warm as she pushed up on tiptoes and wrapped her arms around his neck. This was about wanting and abandon, and she had no intention of fighting it.

Her fingers slipped into his soft hair. She could taste him, smell the peppermint scent of his shampoo.

Sensations bombarded her—the feel of his tongue, the press of his hard body against hers. His mouth and that tiny rumbling sound she heard at the back of his throat.

She'd dreamed about kissing him as a girl but her dreams hadn't felt like this. This was the kiss of a man who wanted a woman. All hot and demanding, smooth and coaxing. It reeled her in.

She wanted more.

That reality hit her like a splash of icy water. It was too much, too soon while the trust between them still stood on shaky ground.

She broke it off and gulped in a huge breath. Let her arms move down to his forearms. "We should…"

He immediately lifted his head and stepped back. "Sorry."

"Don't apologize for that kiss." The heat on her cheeks refused to die down. "It went nuclear faster than I expected."

"Right." His chest lifted and fell in heavy breaths. "I'm going to go."

"Yeah, you should go." But her fingernails dug deeper into his shirt as she held him there.

"You need to let go of me for me to leave."

Her brain battled with her body. There were so many secrets sitting between them. So much she wasn't sure about. Things he might not know that could wreck him. But every time she tried to move away, her hands grabbed on harder. "I don't really want to."

"Good." Then his mouth was on hers again. His tongue slipped over hers as his hand eased just under the hem of her sweater.

He didn't venture higher. He didn't need to because the touch of skin against skin, no matter how innocent or light, had her mind spinning and her stomach dropping to her knees.

Forget the girl crush, she wanted him. Here and now.

That simmering attraction had never gone away.

As soon as she thought it, he lifted his head and rested his forehead against hers. She kept her eyes closed for fear he would see the desire she knew she could not bank. But she could feel his gaze. Feel his thumb as it rubbed against her arm in a soothing gesture that made her want to wrap her body around his and demand he stay.

He breathed in and his whole body moved. "Okay, now I need to go."

"My feelings haven't changed."

"Oh, Hanna." He made a strangled sound. "But you are torn. I can feel it."

He could see it or sense it, she wasn't sure. But in that moment, she was relieved he had more strength than she did.

She sighed. "Yeah."

"Then I have my answer." He kissed her forehead, letting his lips linger before pulling back and looking at her again. "When I stay the night, and I'm hoping that happens soon, it will be because you know you want me to."

"What about you?" Her fingers played with his top button and the sliver of soft skin she could touch at the base of his neck.

"I want to. Trust me." He lifted her hand and kissed the back of it. "Now, good night."

This time he separated their bodies and stepped out of the kitchen. She watched him circle the chair and pick up his jacket off the corner of the couch. She didn't stop him when he took those long confident strides to get to the front door.

"Carter?"

With his hand on the doorknob, he turned around to face her again. "Yeah?"

"Thank you for not being your father."

"You can always count on that to be true." He winked at her, then left.

She wanted to call him back, which was why she didn't. She had decisions to make. Things they needed to talk about.

But one thing was clear: *they* were going to happen soon.

The next afternoon, Carter ventured into the D.C. office. He'd planned to meet Spence at a restaurant for lunch, but Spence texted that he was running late and told Carter to come upstairs for a few minutes.

As soon as he walked into Spence's office, Carter knew he should have seen this coming. Jackson sat there with his feet up on the edge of Spence's desk. They both held files but they were joking about something that didn't sound work related.

"You guys are hard at work, I see." Carter closed the door behind him because these two could say anything.

Spence's smile was almost feral as he put the file down. "Well, well, well. Look who it is. The guy with the big secrets."

Exactly what he'd suspected. Jackson finding out

proved to be a communication line right back to his brothers. "You told him about Hanna."

Spence's smile only grew wider. "Hanna?"

"No, but you just did." Jackson mumbled under his breath about Carter being a dumbass. "I can't believe you fell for that."

Neither could Carter. He must be off his game. He usually stayed ready when it came to his brothers. They were smart and a bit sneaky. If there was information they wanted to know, they were clear that they would use any means to get it out of Carter. In this case, Spence used Jackson.

Spence leaned forward with his hands clasped together. "So, Hanna?"

Jackson nodded. "It's *that* Hanna."

"Hey!" Now he had to fight off both of them. Carter didn't like his odds.

Jackson held up his hands as if in mock surrender. "You already blew it."

"You have Hanna Wilde squirreled away at the house in Virginia? Wait until I tell Derrick." Before Carter could say anything, Spence glanced at Jackson. "Are they having a thing?"

Jackson made that humming sound he always made. "On the verge of it, I'd say."

Since that struck a little too close to the truth, Carter tried to take back the conversation. He dropped into the chair next to Jackson and across from his brother. "She is staying at the cottage."

Spence frowned. "That's a nice nonanswer. Why?"

"Excellent question." Jackson laughed. "Go ahead, Carter. Try to explain this."

"What am I missing?" Spence looked back and

forth between Carter and Jackson. "Is this related to Dad's letter?"

"She didn't want to open it." This time, Carter thought the explanation sounded strange when he said it out loud. When she'd first said it, he got it. He hated being manipulated by his father to do things he didn't want to do and he was related to the man. He couldn't imagine how not interested Hanna would have been in playing Eldrick's games.

"And?" Spence asked.

"She came to the cottage instead." She used the excuse about her father's things, but Carter remembered her mention of a baby. He still didn't know how or where that piece of information fit in and it nagged at him. He'd checked emails and family bank records and...nothing.

Spence opened his hands and shrugged. "Okay, I admit it. I don't get it."

"She needed some time to work out things in her head, things about our dad and hers, and to collect some property. I offered the cottage so she's there—"

"Working things out. Right." Spence broke eye contact with Carter and looked back at Jackson again. "But you think they're having a thing."

Carter missed a lot about hanging out with these two when he was in California, but not this. The ribbing worked great when he wasn't the brother in the firing line, but right now he was and he didn't see that changing any time soon. "I'm standing right here."

"Fine. Are you having a thing with Hanna?" Spence leaned back in his chair. "I'm not judging. I remember she was cute but quiet, and I really liked her dad."

Carter wondered when he'd asked for permission. "Lucky me."

"Hell, I'd like to see you putting down roots, dating, and generally acting like a normal person and not someone who is planning to bolt."

"I'm not going anywhere." Carter repeated the words without thinking. He'd said them so many times to his brothers over the last few months that he was starting to believe them.

"So, you are in a relationship with Hanna or no?" Spence asked the point-blank question without blinking.

Carter picked at the fraying leather seam on the armrest of the chair. "I don't know what we are."

Spence nodded. "So, yes."

"I think it's more of an *almost* thing," Jackson said.

Carter really wanted to ignore both of them but that wasn't easy to do. Neither of them tolerated that sort of thing. Not with all the staring and talking over him and generally making up facts to any questions he refused to answer head-on.

"She's only here on a temporary basis." And that was true. That's what they'd agreed on. But now, saying it, Carter didn't like it. The idea of her picking up and leaving, of not eating meals together. Of not walking the grounds with her, like he did early this morning. His mind rebelled at all of it.

Spence shot Carter a you're-never-going-to-hear-the-end-of-this smile. "Then you, my dear baby brother, need to use some of that charm to get her to stay."

"She has some unfinished business with Dad."
Carter couldn't let himself forget that little fact.

Spence's smile faded. "Don't we all."

Nine

So many secrets swarmed in Hanna's head.

She needed to share at least one of them with Carter. Last night they'd had a close call. She wanted to put the past to the side, if only for a few hours. Being with him, kissing him, felt like the most natural thing ever. But now, in the stark light of day, she thought about his father and hers, her sister, their families, and the baby. That was a lot of baggage piled up around them. Unpacking it seemed like an impossible task.

She used to think Carter knew most of it. That he'd been this carefree playboy who didn't care if he got a woman pregnant. The kind of guy who would send in his rich daddy to clean up his mess. But none of those characteristics fit now.

She sat on the couch, so deep into self-reflection

that she almost didn't hear the knock. She glanced at her cell, expecting to see a text from Carter asking if he could stop by. That's what he did. He checked with her first. But maybe after last night he felt more comfortable stopping by without warning. If so, good.

Their relationship had taken a step forward. The question was how big of a step.

Putting all that aside, she went to the door. She had it open before she remembered the peephole and a lifetime of precautions and generally being smart about her safety. The big fence made an impression, but she'd learned from experience that evil could creep into her life without warning.

All of those things ran through her head as she looked at the two women standing there. The obviously pregnant one with the long brown hair and a pretty round face wore a cute empire-waist dress and a big smile. She also carried a carton with a bakery's name on the side, which made Hanna like her immediately. The other woman, equally stunning in a trim black pantsuit, shifted her weight around, looking far less comfortable about being there.

For a second Hanna couldn't speak. Then she forced out a fumbling greeting. "Uh, hello?"

"I'm Ellie. This is Abby." The pregnant one pointed back and forth with her free hand.

Hanna knew Ellie's name and that she was engaged to Derrick and obviously close to her due date, but none of that explained why they were standing in front of her. "Okay."

Ellie shook the box. "We brought cookies."

Since Ellie was about to be a Jameson by marriage, she'd probably own at least part of the cottage they were standing in. And they looked friendly. Maybe a little sheepish but still welcoming. "You said the magic word. Come in."

Hanna stepped back and let the women move past her. They smelled as nice as they looked. All put together and perfect. Shiny hair, comfortable but stylish looking clothes. Suddenly, Hanna felt like a lump of dirty linen.

She rubbed her hands on the back of her jeans as she followed them to the sitting area. They sat next to each other on the couch. Hanna opted for the safety of the chair across from them because she had a feeling there might be some Carter questions ahead of her.

"So…" The rest of her words died in her throat. That's all she had.

Ellie laughed. "Let me start. I'm engaged to Derrick and clearly pregnant. Seven months, so I have swollen ankles and a permanent case of grumpiness. But the cookies help my mood."

"You hide the bad mood well." All Hanna could see was Ellie's perfect complexion and shiny smile. Nothing seemed forced. She practically radiated happiness. "I figured out from the pregnancy who you were."

Ellie wrestled with the tape that held the box of cookies closed. "Well, we're both pregnant and both engaged to Jameson men, so you get both of us this afternoon."

"You're with Spence?" she asked Abby. Hanna heard her stunned tone and rushed to apologize. "Sorry, I didn't mean to sound so surprised."

But Abby took it in stride. Without breaking eye

contact or showing any sign of being upset, she reached over and snapped the tape Ellie had been picking at, then she smiled at Hanna. A warm, genuine smile. "I'm still trying to believe it, and by 'it' I mean the pregnancy and the engagement. I hadn't really expected either."

Carter had skipped the two future sisters-in-law thing...or had he? Hanna couldn't remember. Their conversations touched on a lot of topics during all those meals together. His upbringing and Eldrick's constantly changing rules. Trips with his brothers. Time with Jackson and his sister. Funny things they all said during the day or did in the past. His thoughts about turning the Virginia property into a business. She loved hearing him talk, having him open up, so she encouraged all of it.

She didn't realize how much she did know until right that second. Somehow, despite her efforts to stay detached, she'd done the opposite. She'd let her defenses drop despite her vows to reinforce them. With the secrets and now the kissing, her mind spun. Being this close to him, this enmeshed in his life, was never the plan. They were not dating. She didn't know what they were, yet this all felt very domestic...and that made her jumpy.

"I think I'm nervous." When Hanna realized she was twisting her hands together until her skin turned white, she grabbed onto the armrests instead.

Abby frowned. "Why?"

"You two are so..." Good grief. They owned mirrors, right? They knew who they were and the kind of family they were marrying into. All that money and power. The potential to get stung by Eldrick and his schemes.

Ellie grabbed a cookie from the now open box. "I'm excited for you to finish that sentence."

That made one of them. Hanna had to fight off the urge to run into the bathroom and throw up.

"We're here because Carter told Spence you were staying here." Abby glanced at Ellie. "Actually, I think Spence tricked him into it." Abby waved a hand in front of her face before continuing again. "Anyway, we know you don't live around here usually and thought you might be lonely, so here we are."

"With cookies." Ellie lifted the box and handed them to Hanna. "They are so good."

Abby winked. "Her favorite."

They had such an easy back-and-forth. The rapport made Hanna miss Gena, or at least miss the relationship she'd always wanted with her sister but never actually had. They were close but Gena could be volatile. Her judgment wasn't great. Carter had been right when he said Gena teetered on the edge of control. Hanna had left because she couldn't watch it…a decision she'd regret forever.

Hanna balanced the box on her lap and glanced up. Ellie and Abby watched her. Ellie wore a soft smile while Abby seemed to be studying and assessing.

None of it made Hanna uncomfortable. The silence did, so she rushed to fill it. "Did you guys grow up with Spence and Derrick?"

Ellie snorted. "Ha! No. I was out of work and hating Derrick when we started dating."

"What?" Hanna tried to remember the gossip she'd read about the couple months ago but she couldn't recall the details. She could see the photos and the locations—expensive hotels and parties. It all fit with the way she'd wanted to see the Jameson brothers before she got to Virginia.

Abby reached over and took a cookie. "I work for Jameson Industries and was about to leave the business because Spence's dad is a piece of garbage."

Some of the tension running through Hanna eased. She didn't realize how stiff she'd been holding her shoulders until Abby made the comment. "Man, he really is."

"We also have an ulterior motive for our visit." Abby pointed at Hanna with her cookie. "We wanted to meet you."

Hanna couldn't imagine their lives. Probably filled with parties and business functions. The idea of them thinking about her, even for a second, confused her. "Why?"

"Because of Carter," Ellie said.

Abby nodded. "You guys are together and we love Carter—"

Just as she feared. "No."

"Excuse me?" Abby's eyebrow lifted and for a second she sounded like the tough businesswoman Hanna imagined her to be.

Carter. Talk about a tough conversation. She'd been thinking about him nonstop. About that kiss, about how good his hands felt on her. She wished she could write him off; she needed to because being with him meant spilling so many secrets and trusting him. A voice in her head screamed a warning at the thought of doing either. "There's not… We're not… I mean, there was kissing and…ugh."

A huge smile broke over Abby's face. "That sounds so familiar."

"Right?" Ellie shook her head as she took a bite of her cookie. "Those Jameson men."

They lost her. Hanna had no idea what they were talking about. "What do you mean?"

Abby sighed as she put down the cookie she'd been holding but not eating. "The Jameson men have the power to get the most stable woman turned around and babbling."

Exactly. That description totally made sense to Hanna. She'd been off balance and stumbling ever since Carter showed up at her door. It was nice to know she wasn't alone. Sounded as if this was a regular affliction. "Have you met Carter's other girlfriends?"

"I like that you used the word *other*." Abby flashed a smile.

Hanna couldn't imagine Spence having any defense to that look. Hanna couldn't find one. "I didn't mean—"

"But no. He's charming and very sweet and funny, but also very private." Ellie's head tilted to the side. "Hence, our curiosity about you."

The women had been there fifteen minutes and Hanna already liked them. They were open and friendly. They searched for information but didn't try to hide their snooping with games. Hanna got the very real sense the visit came out of a love for Carter and a need to see where she fit into his life.

She guessed Jackson was to blame for planting that wrong seed…and it was wrong. It had to be because with their families and their pasts their lives couldn't intersect like that.

Disappointment slammed into her. Her chest ached and she had to ball her hands into fists to keep from rubbing the spot. For a few seconds—a flash only—she wondered what it would be like to be with Carter, to be the one he built a life with. She blinked out the thought as soon as it formed in her head.

"I don't want to disappoint you, but we're really not *together* together."

Silence buzzed through the room. Both Ellie and Abby stayed quiet. They watched her, but Hanna didn't sense pity or anger. After a few beats of quiet, Ellie looked at Abby and nodded.

Ellie turned back to Hanna. "But you still need company...or would you rather we leave?"

Now that they were here, she didn't want them to go. Hanna couldn't really explain it. She didn't have a lot of friends. Over the last year, she'd been mourning her sister and the baby, she'd been avoiding Eldrick, and hadn't had the time or emotional strength to be a great friend to anyone. She hadn't realized how much she missed the comfort of friends until now.

She shrugged. "I kind of want to hear why Abby hates Eldrick Jameson."

"Done." Abby stood up. "Let's get some drinks and napkins to go with the cookies, then I'll tell you all about how he made a pass at me in an effort to derail my relationship with Spence."

Hanna started to stand up, then fell back into her chair as Abby talked. "Are you kidding?"

Ellie snorted. "Oh, Hanna. We have so many Eldrick stories. The lies. The things he's making his sons do so that Derrick can officially run the company he already runs. You don't even have to share yours. You can just enjoy ours."

"He really is awful." Normally, Hanna wouldn't be so quick to share her true feelings, but she felt perfectly safe making that statement with this audience.

Abby stood in the middle of the kitchen. "Help me with those napkins and we'll fill you in on our experiences."

Hanna wasn't about to say no to that offer.

Later that night, Carter stood in Hanna's kitchen, holding a cup of decaf. He stopped in the middle of drinking when Hanna dropped her big news. "Wait, you had cookies with Ellie and Abby today?"

She slid onto the bar stool across from him with a warm smile. "Weird, right?"

Carter waited for the blood to rush back to his head. The women he considered family had rushed over to talk to Hanna. He assumed he could thank Spence for that, but later, because right now a million questions filled his head.

"Not really. I guess." While he was skeptical about the visit, he didn't want Hanna to think anything but good things about Ellie and Abby. He loved them and couldn't imagine either one of his brothers getting through the rest of their lives without them. But he barely knew his place in the family. The idea of bringing Hanna into the mess didn't make sense to him, especially when he wasn't sure what they meant to each other, if anything. "They likely came out because they were worried you'd meet Derrick and Spence first and then take off."

Hanna played with the fringe on the edge of the place mat, slipping the material through her fingers with precision. "I don't remember them being that scary."

Her nonanswer stopped him. Of course she would leave. They technically weren't dating. Hell, he didn't even know if he planned on sticking around much past Ellie giving birth. But they'd originally talked about her staying a few days and they'd blown by that deadline. The usual pressing need to move on hadn't hit him. He didn't want to think that was due to her, but he started to wonder. "Are you going to?"

She shrugged. "There's much we need to talk about."

The contents of the envelope. The mention of the baby. The secrets were starting to pile up. Still, he didn't want to push because he didn't want to push her away. "You have to stick around for that."

"So do you, which sounds like it could be a problem." She flipped the material around a few more times, then flattened it against the counter under her palm. "Your future sisters-in-law think you're going to bolt once Ellie's baby is born. They didn't say they worried about it, but I could tell they want you here. In fact, I think Ellie would be happier if you lived with them, like Spence did."

That must have been a hell of a talk. He'd been trying for days, and Ellie and Abby came in, offering cookies, and got more than he had. He didn't like that feeling of once more being on the outside looking in. "She's in nesting mode."

"It's more than that. She said she didn't want to

freak you out, but she hated the idea of you moving on once Eldrick turned the business over to Derrick."

"Yes, I'll go, and Spence will work there. I'd get the benefit of their hard labor." He thought about how crappy that sounded. It was one thing to be the brother who schmoozed people. It was another not to contribute. "That was my original plan."

"But now?" She stared at him, head-on and no flinching.

He met her stare for stare. He decided not to answer the unspoken question about them because he didn't know what they were or even if they were a "they." "Nothing is as clear as it was a few weeks ago."

"We met a few weeks ago."

She was pushing and his usual reaction would be to pull away. He clamped down on that instinct and stepped closer to the counter. Reached across until his hand covered hers. "That's kind of my point."

For a few seconds, they stood there with music softly playing in the background. He caressed the back of her hand with his thumb. Felt a burst of energy arc between them.

Her second hand joined her first until she cradled his fingers in all of hers. "What would you say if I asked you to stay here tonight?"

His heartbeat thundered in his ears until he could barely hear. "I'd force myself to stop and try to figure out if you're still conflicted."

"Not about this part. Not anymore."

That sounded so good but he still needed to be sure. "The other stuff, the things that are worrying you, can they wait?"

"They've already waited a long time."

He wasn't convinced that was the right answer. Everything between them felt…unsettled. Hot and full of need but a little off, as if they should just get to it and deal with the consequences. His father, Gena. That stupid envelope.

Before he could launch into the first topic, she walked around the counter. Never broke eye contact with him. Held his hand as she stepped in front of him with the other hand resting on his hip. "Hi, there."

"Hi."

"You going to run on me, Carter?"

The risks were high but right then, in that moment, none of them mattered. "I couldn't, even if I wanted to."

Need pounded through him. Everything about her intrigued him. Her voice, her body, that smile. He loved to listen to her, talk with her, share things. None of that matched with the guy he thought he was, the one who ran instead of staying to take the heat. He liked certainty and clarity and very few ties. He liked to breeze through without getting involved. The comfort that came with keeping things easy and shallow. But she blurred every part of his life. Shook it up and left him fighting for balance.

And that was without touching him.

But she touched him now. She slid her hand up his side and every nerve ending ignited. Muscles strained at the soft brush of her fingers.

His arm slipped around her and he tugged her closer. His lips brushed her cheek and he felt a shiver run through her. So sexy and it only spurred him on.

His mouth skimmed the side of her face to her ear. He licked around the outside and her body fell harder against his.

"Yes." Her breath blew across his neck.

It was his turn to tremble. He couldn't hide the small shake in his hands as he held her. A voice in his head screamed *now.*

So much had happened, so many questions and half answers that he needed them to be clear on this. "Tell me to stop if you want me to stop. No questions asked. I'll go back to the main—"

"Carter?"

He watched her, waiting. "Yeah?"

"Stop talking." Her hand slipped lower, right to the top of his butt.

She couldn't be clearer than that. "Yes, ma'am."

He shut his mind off and kissed her. Poured all his desire and need into it. Let her feel how much he wanted to be with her, to touch her. He didn't hold back or play games because he didn't want to. Not with her.

Any hope of staying detached fizzled. His mouth covered hers and the heat sparked between them. Her hands slipped into his hair and his hands roamed over her back.

They touched everywhere.

He could smell her and hear her. Feel her. It was better than the dreams he'd been having about her, and those had been pretty great except for the part where he woke up alone and sweating.

He pulled her in until their bodies rubbed against each other. The friction had his brain misfiring but he managed to walk them out of the kitchen. He eased her back, guiding her through the living room, around the coffee table and chair, to the bedroom door. With every step he kissed her. Their mouths met in a series of breathtaking kisses that nearly knocked the knees out from under him.

Through it all he held her, cradled her against his chest as his mouth skimmed over her sexy neck. He didn't bother to look around. He spied the bed out of the corner of his eye and that was good enough.

He kept moving, spinning them around until the backs of his knees hit the mattress. Sliding down, he opened his legs and pulled her to stand between them. The position put his mouth even with her stomach. He leaned in and pressed a kiss against her shirt. Felt the muscles underneath jump in response.

Being this close to her, wanting her, humbled him. He didn't race or throw her down. Not when he wanted to savor every second. Wanted to unwrap her like she was a present he never thought he'd get. When she reached down and again tangled her fingers in his hair he couldn't help but lean into the touch.

His control hovered right at the edge. It blinked out on him a few times when he pressed his cheek against her stomach. He smoothed his hand up and down the backs of her thighs. "You feel so good."

Her breathing kicked up under his ear. Those hands, soft yet strong, trailed down his back. He lifted her then. Scooped her up and dragged her around him. He didn't let go until her back hit the bed and then he crawled over her. Slipped up her body, loving the feel of how they fit together.

When he reached into his back pocket and took out

the condom he'd put there in the hope he might need it tonight, she nodded. Balancing on his elbows with an arm on each side of her head, he looked down. Ran his fingertips over her bottom lip as he thought about how good it felt to kiss her. Then he did. He bent down and pressed his mouth against hers. This kiss was slow and deliberate, a promise of what was to come.

When they broke apart she lifted her hand and caressed his cheek. "The answer is still yes."

He couldn't help but laugh at that. "Thank goodness."

Her fingers traveled down his chest, undoing each button as she went. She had his shirt open and slid her hands inside, tunneling under his white T-shirt to bare skin. The touch was electric. It made his heart pound and his mouth go dry. Every ounce of common sense abandoned him.

His head dipped again and this time he didn't stop. His mouth followed his hands as he pushed her sweater up. With a lift of her upper body, she helped him shove it off and onto the floor. Something he'd worry about tomorrow morning. Right now, he had other things on his mind, like enjoying the touch of his lips against her skin.

He kissed and caressed her. Slipped his palms over her breasts, loving the shape of her. He kissed her through her bra. Licked her until her back arched and she whispered his name. He'd never heard anything so sexy. Never been so ready.

Sitting up, he tore off his shirt and his hands went to his jeans. But she beat him there. Her fingers worked on the button and his zipper. The sound of it coming down screeched through the room but he blocked it out. This was about them and her breathing and the way the light hit her bare skin. He'd stripped off her top and unhooked her bra. Now he slipped it off her shoulders, letting it fall until she grabbed it in front of her and ripped it off.

He wanted to reach down and touch her again but his brain wouldn't send out the signal, not when Hanna slipped her hand inside his jeans. But who could blame him? She cupped him, caressed him with an expert hand. Her fingers danced over him, making his hips tip forward, then she tightened her hold.

Every brush of her fingers and the heavy breaths escaping her made him ache. He wanted to touch her, press his body against hers. When she put her hands on his hips and brought him against her again, he didn't fight it. He let her coax him closer. Enjoyed the way her hand slid over his length. Counting to ten while she did it over and over again.

But he couldn't wait any longer.

Pressing her back into the mattress, he stood up long enough to strip off his jeans and briefs. Then he was back. He sat between her legs, unzipping her pants and sliding them down. Slowly peeling them off her and taking the lacy black bikini bottoms with them.

When there was nothing between them, he kissed her again. He licked her bottom lip, nipped at the top. Felt his stomach flip over when she dragged him in for a kiss that blew out any doubt he ever had that they would end up like this.

He swept his hand down her body, loving the

curve of her stomach and the softness of her thigh. Without him saying a word, she bent her leg and dropped it to the side. The shift gave him the access he wanted. His finger slipped over her, inside her. And when her head fell back, he took advantage of the position and skimmed his mouth down her neck to the inviting dip at the base of her throat.

With each pass of his hand, her body opened for him, readied for him until he didn't think he could wait one more second. Once again, she was there, dragging the condom from where he'd dropped it and handing it to him. Not saying a word as she trailed her fingers over his bottom lip.

He lifted his hips, separating from her only long enough to roll the condom on. Then he was back, easing inside her. Her internal muscles tightened around him, pulsed against him. He dragged in a hard breath, trying to regain his balance from the sensations pummeling him. But she wouldn't let him stop. She lifted her hips and he was done.

His body took over. The steady in and out. The way her body held him, wrapped around him. He couldn't think and gasped as he tried to drag in enough air. Their breaths mixed and echoed throughout the room. He pushed in and pulled out. Let her set the rhythm.

When her fingers clamped on his waist, he moved faster. One hand eased between their damp bodies. He touched her then and her mouth dropped open. She tensed under him and he knew she was close.

He whispered her name.

With a rough gulp of breath, she reached for him. Brought his mouth down for one more kiss. Broke it off as her mouth opened and her head tilted back. He watched, fascinated, as the orgasm moved through her. Her body shook and her legs clenched against his hips. She was strong and beautiful, so hot that she stole his breath.

Then it was his turn. He tried to hold it off, to savor every second, but his body had other ideas. His eyes slipped shut as his hips bucked. His body moved and shifted as the last of the pulses moved through him.

The orgasm zapped his strength and his arms gave out. He caught his weight in time, before he crushed her. Managed to slide slightly to the side.

Lying half on her, half next to her, he slid his arm over her stomach and pulled her close as he tried to calm his heart. It thumped so hard he half expected to see it move in his chest.

"Wow." She said the word without opening her eyes.

His smile was automatic. "You get all the credit."

She turned her head and looked at him then. "We were pretty fantastic together."

Whatever she wanted to say, fine, but he knew the truth. She got the credit here. He found the energy to place a soft kiss on her shoulder. "And you are my inspiration."

"I like that." She fully rolled on to her side. "I like you."

Any chance at sleep vanished. All he wanted was to lie there, looking at her. "You're stunning."

"And you, Carter Jameson, need to rest." She smiled when he groaned. "I hope you brought another condom."

He held up two fingers. "That's it."

She pushed him to his back and slid over him. "After that we'll have to get creative."

He was wide-awake now. For the first in a long time, running was the last thing on his mind. "Lucky for you, I'm very creative."

"I'm counting on that."

Ten

Three days later, Hanna looked around the rectangular table in the Virginia estate's dining room. The fancy glittering chandelier hanging over the centerpiece likely cost more than most homes, and that was saying something in the D.C. metro area. Gold wallpaper gave the room a bright, sunny look despite the gray day outside. Glasses clanked together and bowls and plates of food traveled around from one person to the next.

The steady hum of conversation echoed in her head. She'd formally met everyone here before this big family dinner, except Spence and Derrick, but she knew them from when they were all much younger. Despite being the new person in the room, they treated her like an old friend. Jackson and Spence joked with her. Ellie coddled Hanna with an overprotective mothering instinct. Abby spent most of her time shaking her head at all of the antics.

Hanna really identified with Abby.

When Jackson brought up some story about a lie Spence told as a kid to hide the fact he crashed a car, Derrick almost spit out his food laughing. Even Ellie lost it when hearing about those days.

Hanna leaned closer to Carter. "How did you talk me into this?"

"Blame Ellie and Abby. They are relentless."

Jackson leaned across Carter to talk with Hanna. "Are you trying to hide something?"

That earned him a tap on the side of the head from Carter. "Go away."

Hanna knew it could not have hurt but the fake stunned expression Jackson wore made her laugh. "Be nice to Jackson."

He winked at her. "Listen to your woman."

The table conversation picked that moment to stop. Everyone looked at her. There were smiles all around, the annoying kind that made her want to kick Carter for getting her into this. They had fallen into some sort of relationship but a big family dinner made what they had seem important. She couldn't think about that, not when Carter had emphasized his lifetime of keeping things shallow.

The clinking sound reminded Hanna of a wedding. She felt the rush of a headache a second later.

Derrick changed the subject by clearing his throat. "We wanted to make sure Carter was feeding you. That's why we're all here, at this house I despise."

Ellie slipped her hand over Derrick's. "And we wanted you to know we'd like to spend time with you."

"Yeah, Carter. We want to see her, too." Spence toasted Carter, then took a long sip of water.

Carter glared back. "You can shut up any time now."

With that, the conversation kicked up again. The brothers talked across the table to each other. Ellie rolled her eyes. The scene didn't amount to a food fight, or even veer out of control, because Hanna doubted Ellie would tolerate that, but it did steer close to the edge. So much noise and talking.

Memories plowed into her. The days filled with talking to Carter and walking the estate grounds. The nights spent cuddled together, touching and learning each other's bodies. The whispers, the joking. The way he kissed her…everywhere.

Then her mind traveled back to those dinners with her dad when he tried so hard to fix the things his young daughters would eat. How he would talk with Gena for what felt like hours to calm her down when she got so upset over unimportant things she viewed as slights. It all came flooding back to Hanna and she waited for the guilt to hit her. She was with the people who she'd believed made her family miserable, but in that moment all she felt was a sadness that her family couldn't be there, too.

She knew from Carter that Eldrick had never allowed talking at the table, not from his sons. Hanna assumed the thunderous noise now was a reaction to that past. It struck her as a right time to ask the question that had been poking at her since they all arrived. "Is Jackson a family name?"

Carter stopped talking to Spence and smiled at

her. "Nice pivot. It's always a good idea to throw the attention on to someone else."

"I just wondered." Anxiety shot through her. She had a reason to ask. Those notes in her father's journal.

The suggestion that Eldrick kept the ultimate secret.

Jackson swallowed the chicken he was eating and put his fork down on the side of his plate. "My mom's name is Jackie. She didn't want a mini-me, so my twin sister—"

"Who is awesome," Spence slipped in.

Jackson nodded but never broke eye contact with Hanna. "Her name is Zoe. I got the version of Jackie."

Carter stared at Jackson. "I didn't know that."

"Wait." Derrick lowered his water glass to the table. "You're sharing family secrets now, after we've asked for years. That and the fact Hanna has gotten Carter to settle down for five minutes makes me think she has superpowers."

Jackson shrugged. "Not all of us have colorful families like you guys."

The conversation stayed light. And then Ellie looked straight at Hanna. "How is the cottage?"

"You're not staying at the main house?" Spence jumped in his seat, then glared at Abby next to him. "Ouch! What was that for?"

"Be decent," she said at a near whisper.

"Is it a secret they're sleeping together?" Jackson asked.

Hanna felt the tension now. It ratcheted up inside her. Not that she was embarrassed. The fear was about the lack of boundaries. If this topic was okay for the table, she hated to think what might be next.

She shot Carter a side look. "Are all of your family dinners like this?"

Carter nodded. "Yes."

"Unfortunately," Jackson said at the same time.

Carter slipped an arm over the back of her chair. His fingers slid into her hair. "If you want to go or—"

"It's fine." Being with him anchored her just as panic started to rise in her belly. The touch should have had the opposite effect, made her more tense and worried, but it didn't.

After a lifetime of quiet and calm dinners, this rowdy one actually invigorated her. But a wave of guilt hit her, too. They were nice and friendly and she knew things...things she didn't think they knew. Things she *knew* Carter had never learned. She didn't know when or even how to spill them. It really wasn't her place, but she knew and being with him, even temporarily, meant she had some responsibility for him.

"Maybe if you weren't sitting on top of her," Spence said before he popped a green bean in his mouth.

Derrick frowned at Carter. "Yeah, do you need a bigger chair?"

"For goodness' sake." Ellie sighed. "Don't you start."

Jackson laughed. "You heard the pregnant woman. Be nice to your brother."

"We have a lot of pregnant women at the table." Spence jerked in his chair a second time before he glared at Abby. "Again? I meant you and Ellie. I don't know if—" This time he shifted to the side. "Do not kick me again."

"Then stop talking," Abby said through clenched teeth.

The conversation continued to unravel. They talked for a few minutes about the habits of pregnant women, then moved on to how much of an emotional wreck Derrick had been when he found out Ellie's pregnancy was high risk because it had happened while she had an IUD.

The topics swirled around Hanna. She heard bits and pieces. Even as they moved on to something that happened at work and a discussion about the best kind of cheesecake, the truth weighed down on her and her mind stayed on babies. On pregnancy. On all the things she hadn't told Carter.

His fingers slipped through her hair, then massaged the back of her neck, as if he could sense her growing anxiety. The move, so sweet, felt comfortable and intimate. Something a boyfriend might do, like bringing her to a family dinner.

The dizziness hit her out of nowhere. The room began to spin and her stomach flipped with it. The voices blurred in her head as the guilt crushed her into the chair.

She'd never asked to be pulled into this family's drama. Carter had offered her a chance to search for her dad's journal. She thought she could look for answers and be left alone. Somewhere along the line, all of that changed.

A lump formed in her throat. She clutched her napkin on her lap with both hands. She could hear her breathing. It sounded so loud in her ears. The rush in and out. She didn't know how they couldn't hear it. She thought someone called her name. Carter's fingers stilled. The ramp-up of noise turned to a scream in her head.

She had to get up.

She stumbled, trying to find her footing and unable to make her legs move. "I can't do this."

After balancing her hands on the table, she stood. Took a part of the tablecloth with her, rattling all the dishes.

Carter's voice cut off in the middle of whatever conversation he was having. "Hey."

She couldn't answer him. Not now. She had to get out of that room, maybe the state. When her balance faltered, Carter stood up next to her, keeping her on her feet.

His arm wrapped around her. "Are you okay?"

"No."

"What's wrong?" Concern vibrated in his voice and showed in every line of his face.

His tone—all that worry was genuine and sweet... and sent a new wave of guilt crashing over her. She couldn't look around the table out of fear of what she'd see. "All of them. You."

Carter made an odd noise. "I know it's a lot of people, but they mean well."

"It's not that." She shook her head, trying to force the words back. This was not the time or place. Talking now would be unfair to Carter. He might be close to his brothers, but he deserved privacy.

"Hanna, talk to me."

The truth was right there. She bit her bottom lip to hold the words in. But a quick look at Jackson's face told her she needed to say something. He looked half ready to lunge across the table and comfort her. They all did.

She turned to Carter, tried to face only him. Her fingers dug into his arm but he didn't make a sound.

"I… You weren't supposed to be this guy."

Along with all her other mistakes, believing the worst about him had been one of her biggest. Without that, none of this would have happened. She would have gone to him with the truth, been on his side against his father. Not expected him to be a version of Eldrick. "You were supposed to be a jerk. Rich and entitled. Someone who did awful things, then moved on and let other people fix everything for you."

He frowned. "I thought we already went through this."

"Gena." It's the only word Hanna could get out.

Carter's mouth opened and closed a few times before he started talking again. "Hanna, I promise you that was a fling. Short. It meant nothing to either of us."

"Wait, Gena?" Spence asked.

Carter ignored his brother, put his hands on her arms in a loose hold and stared at her. The look was intense and desperate, as if he needed her to listen. "I've been honest with you about Gena and—"

Not again. She put her hand over his mouth. "I haven't."

"What?"

She couldn't lie to him for one more second. The words spilled out on a rush of pain and regret as she dropped her hand. "She was pregnant, Carter."

His head snapped back. "What are you talking about?"

"The two of you. Gena. After that weekend together."

She heard a male voice. Someone swore, but none of them moved.

Carter shook his head. "Not possible. We used protection."

"I was there. She was definitely pregnant." There were so many details. Hanna wasn't sure what mattered right now. "She didn't know at first, not for many months, but then she got sick and kept getting sick. Then the weight gain."

"I don't..." Carter continued to shake his head as his gaze switched to Derrick, then Spence. "No."

She knew he needed to talk with the people he loved, get their support, but she had to tell him this one last part. Make him understand why she'd made the choices she'd made.

"Your father showed up and threatened her. Made it clear she wasn't getting into the Jameson family that way."

"He didn't know about Gena. He couldn't..." Carter just stopped talking.

Hanna took that as a sign to continue even though her stomach ached and her head pounded. "Maybe he had you followed. Honestly, she may have called him and begged for money. I really don't know anymore, except that it's clear you didn't send him to keep me quiet like I once believed."

"Is that when she killed herself?" Jackson asked in a soft voice.

He knew. Of course he knew. Hanna realized for

the first time that Jackson was likely the person in the office who had investigated her for Carter after that first night in New York. "A month later."

Carter shook his head. "While she was still pregnant."

It wasn't a question, so she didn't answer out loud except to nod.

Derrick closed his eyes. "Damn."

"What did Dad want?" Spence asked.

She answered him but kept her focus on Carter. She could feel his fingers loosen on her arms and guessed he'd gone numb. "For her to go away."

"The baby…" Carter looked away from her, then back again. "Hanna, I didn't—"

"He came to me after she died. Threatened me not to find you or say anything. Gave me a check to stay quiet." She hadn't taken it, but she doubted that mattered right now. "I'm sorry."

Spence snorted. "Why are you sorry?"

"That's Dad's screwup, not yours," Jackson said.

The support sent a rush of relief through her, but she couldn't enjoy it. She wasn't ready for forgiveness or understanding. And she noticed Carter wasn't the one offering it.

She wanted him to know her side. "I didn't tell you because I thought you knew and didn't care. It's why I pushed you away when you first found me. Why I didn't want to open that envelope."

"I had no idea about any of this."

She touched his cheek. "I know that now."

A chair screeched against the hardwood floor as Derrick stood up. "You're saying Dad threatened Gena and then he threatened you."

"He talked about saving the family name and not allowing some maid to ruin everything." She looked at the rest of them then. "That's what I do. I'm sure you know, but in case you don't, I clean houses. I'm not a business executive."

Ellie shot her an odd look. "Do you think we care about that?"

That's just it, she didn't think they cared. Now that she knew them, spent time with them, saw them as adults separate from Eldrick, she saw them as warm and welcoming. Just like Carter. So, she didn't hold back. She tried to put it all out there.

"Hanna." Carter's voice stayed low and sounded a bit unsteady.

He would lose it now. Yell at her. She deserved it for holding back for weeks, but she couldn't stand there and listen to his anger. Having him be mad at her made something inside her shrink.

"I'm sorry." She shook her head, silently begging him to believe her. "I know you're not your father, Carter. You're a little lost and fighting to figure out who you are in this family. From what I see, you fit here. You're loved and respected."

Spence scoffed. "Of course he is."

She couldn't continue to stand there, looking at Carter's broken expression. She turned to the rest of the table. Forced her chin to stay up and forced herself to meet their eyes. "I didn't mean to lie to you guys or..." Her gaze stopped on Ellie. "You're all so nice. I keep waiting for you to be something else but it doesn't happen."

Derrick exhaled as he put a hand on the back of Ellie's chair. "Hanna, go ahead and sit down."

Ellie gave her a smile. "Yes, this is Eldrick's mess, not yours."

"And mine." Carter's voice dipped even lower. The despair lingered in every word.

Derrick winced. "Carter, come on."

"Gena was pregnant by me. She killed herself after Dad threatened her." He looked at Hanna. "No wonder you hated me."

But that was excatly wrong. All that anger hid the wanting she'd ignored for so long. They spent time together and what she felt for him, that blinding attraction, changed and swelled. It grew until it overtook everything else. Until the last of her control snapped and she tumbled and fell.

She could see it now. The truth rushed in on her, threatening to bowl her over.

"I wanted to but couldn't. Now I look at you and I see so much more than even you see. I want to be with you. Spend time with you. I think I'm falling for you. Love, Carter. Not sex. Not temporary." That truth slipped out right as it formed in her head.

She'd been fighting and making excuses, but the reality was she didn't need to be in Virginia. She stayed because of him. She wrestled with secrets and ran the risk of being on Eldrick's stomping grounds for Carter. He was worth it.

Jackson's eyes widened. "That's new information."

"What did you just say?" Carter's hand slipped to her chin as he forced her to return his gaze. "Hanna?"

She couldn't stay there one more second. It was all

too soon, too much. She'd barely been able to process her feelings before broadcasting them. "I'm sorry."

Then she ran out of the room.

Eleven

Carter reached for Hanna as she rushed out of the room. He missed her and his hand knocked against the sideboard. He didn't even feel it. He didn't feel anything. His mind raced, unable to hold on to any thought for more than a second.

But then Jackson was at his side. "Hey, take a breath."

"She said love." Carter doubled over, unable to finish. "And there was a baby."

Love. Responsibility. A pregnancy he never knew about. It all clashed together in his head. He'd felt a pull toward Hanna from the minute he saw her in New York. He knew she was hiding things from him. That ticked him off and made him want to know more. Now that he did he felt sick. He lost a baby without ever knowing it. He played a role, however small, in Hanna's loss of her sister.

He and his father.

"I know. I got it," Derrick said. "We all did."

Carter dropped into the nearest chair. "Everything is upside down."

Spence shook his head. "Not you. You're still rock-solid."

Carter appreciated the support but right now all he wanted to do was leave. Old instincts kicked in and shouted at him to get out. Only this time he could block them, tone them down. For now. "I don't feel that way."

Jackson sat down next to Carter and rested his hand on the back of his chair. "What would you have done if you'd known?"

Carter could barely think and Jackson was giving him a quiz. "What?"

"If Gena had told you. What would you have done?" Jackson held up a hand. "Don't think about it. Just answer."

Carter's brain scrambled. It was as if he'd been thrown back in time and confronted with the problem. "Convince her to move back here. Try to get to know her better. Make sure she got care and ask you guys to help me make her feel welcome."

Derrick came around the table to stand on the other side of Carter. "Okay, let's—"

"We barely knew each other. It was a weekend fling. Not like what I feel for Hanna." The words echoed inside him. Settled in. Everything was different with Hanna. Part of him knew it but now the reality beat inside his brain until he couldn't think of anything else.

Derrick nodded. "Then you have your answer."

Carter had lost the trail of the conversation. "What does that mean?"

"You wouldn't have pushed Gena away or ignored your responsibilities. You would not have run." Jackson leaned in. "And now you know that you get the difference between doing what's right and being in love."

"You're giving me too much credit."

Jackson took a deep breath. "As an outsider—"

Spence jumped in. "You're not that."

"Fine. As a non-Jameson, let me suggest a few things." Jackson looked around the room. "First, you're all too fertile and should think about different birth control."

Abby sighed. "I wish I could argue with that."

"And, you're also the best men I know despite being the offspring of one of the worst."

"Also true," Ellie agreed, leaning back in her chair.

"You have a lot of guilt and other crap to wade through, Carter," Derrick added, "but there is a woman at that cottage who loves you and is hurting as much as you are. If I were you, I'd go to her."

Yes, he needed to go to her. But he wasn't sure he was ready.

She'd held back information. But could he blame her? Thinking he was like Eldrick, that Carter had orchestrated his father's maneuvering, wasn't really a stretch. He and his father both acted one way in public and another in private. Carter could understand how she might have twisted that around to think he *was* his dad. Add in Gena's tendency to exaggerate and it was a miracle he'd convinced Hanna to come to Virginia.

Unbelievable that Hanna had trusted him enough to sleep with him.

"How could she not blame me?" He wasn't searching for an answer. He just needed to ask the question out loud.

Jackson grimaced and looked to Spence.

He nodded and then started talking. "I'm guessing she did, but now she knows better. Eventually, you will, as well."

Ellie made a grumbling noise before she stood up and walked around the table. She gave Jackson a gentle shove to move him out of the way. Then she sat down next to Carter, ignoring everyone else in the room. "Carter, you know I love you, right?"

"Is there a *but* coming?"

"But right now, Hanna needs you. The two of you can figure this out together, but you need to talk." She reached over and squeezed his hand. "Go do that."

Jackson laughed. "Listen to the wise pregnant woman."

"You should always listen to the women in the family." Then Ellie looked around, as if challenging the men to question her.

Abby nodded. "Exactly."

"And while you're doing that we'll plot how to make Dad pay for this." There was no amusement in Derrick's voice. The flat line of his mouth suggested he wasn't kidding.

The thought of them all ganging up on their father was the one light moment in this conversation. The mental image would fuel him for a long time.

"I want a part in that, so don't start without me."

She should pack.

The thought ran through Hanna's head as she sat down on the edge of the couch. She'd told the truth, delivered the bad news. She was nothing more than a messenger, but she would pay for this.

The way she'd told him, right in front of everyone. Not in the quiet of the bedroom after they'd had sex or during one of the many times they'd sat and talked together as they ate. Nope, she'd blurted it out. Made a spectacle of an already difficult situation.

How could she ever trust him? She'd likely killed any feelings or attraction he ever felt for her, and that possibility made her stomach roll. She wrapped her arms around her middle and tried to fight her way through the painful darkness falling over her.

"Hanna."

She looked up to see Carter standing in the doorway to the cottage. She'd been so lost in thought she didn't hear him come in. Even now, he only hovered without coming in.

Pain and confusion thrummed off him. She'd done that to him. She tried to think of a way to make some part of this better but nothing came to her except the obvious. "I'm sorry."

"My father…"

"Is not you." That point was so clear in her head now. She wished she'd understood it earlier. "You didn't do anything except go to California, and that had been your plan all along. You weren't running."

"I was running from him, from the family name."
He shook his head. "Not from her and the baby."

"I swear to you I do know that now." The air in the
room nearly choked Hanna. It felt thick as it passed
through her raw throat. She half wished she could
yell and cry and get it all out. That losing it would
bring her some strange measure of control. "Do you
want me to go?"

She hadn't found the strength to stand up, but
she'd walk out, find another place to wait out the
suffocating sadness that threatened to swamp her.
She had her father's journal. She could copy it and
send it to Carter. Maybe that would explain a little
more about why she was so skeptical of his family.

His mouth twisted in a frown. "Why would I?"

"I kept this from you, and other things, then I
told you this heartbreaking thing in the least private
way possible."

And it *was* heartbreaking to Carter. She could see
it in the paleness of his face and the way his eyes
had dimmed. It was as if the life had run right out of
him when he'd found out he'd almost been a father
and never known.

Some guys would celebrate the near miss. Write
Gena off as a bad decision and be more careful next
time. But Carter seemed to feel the gravity of what
had happened in every muscle. It confirmed what she
already knew—what he seemed to not get—that he
was one of the good guys.

Despite his father and the cold upbringing and
feeling like the "extra" son, he was a good man.

"Hanna." He finally stepped inside and shut the
cottage door behind him. He'd left his coat up at the

main house and the wind had blown his hair until it stuck up in places. "You're not Gena."

"What?"

"You're not a stand-in for her. My feelings for you have nothing to do with that weekend with her. And you weren't responsible for her decisions. Knowing you, you tried to save her and are kicking yourself because you didn't do enough."

"She drove that car off a bridge." Hanna choked back a sob. "And I wasn't there to stop her."

"If you had stopped her then, there probably would have been a next time." He walked over and sat on the couch beside her. "Her decision wasn't about you. Hell, it might not even have been about Eldrick, though I'm sure he played a role in it."

Hanna stared down at her lap, at her folded hands as she dug her nails into her skin. The pinch didn't even register in her brain. All she heard was the sound of his soothing voice, sad but clear, as the coolness of the outside thrummed off him.

He put his hand under her chin and forced her to look at him. "We're—the two of us and what's been happening there—not about her. Not at all."

The distance between them, though small, proved to be too much. She wrapped her arms around him and held on. She'd admitted something so big, so overwhelming and seemingly impossible as her love for him. She didn't expect him to say it back, not with all the confusion swirling around them. But he held on to her. He didn't shove her away and move on, and right now that's all that mattered to her.

She wasn't sure how long they sat there. She didn't want to let him go. The vulnerability she felt... She focused on her breathing, on the feel of his warm skin beneath her hand, the sound of his heartbeat.

When she opened her eyes again, they were lying on the couch on their sides, with his chest against her back and his arm anchoring them in place.

She almost laughed at how right it felt.

In the silence, she matched her breathing to his. Brushed her fingers over the back of his hand, loving the feel of his lean muscles. Her skin tingled from the puffs of air blowing across the back of her neck.

Suddenly, she was very aware of him. Of every single part of him.

"I want to be close to you."

His lips lingered at her ear. "Me, too."

He exhaled and she felt the move through her body.

They touched everywhere. Tangled legs and arms resting on each other, holding each other.

"I've made a lot of mistakes." He pushed her hair off her face. "Serious ones. Ones that hurt people."

"I've made mistakes, too." Sometimes there were no good answers.

"I've watched my father's manipulations, and I haven't always stepped in."

"I came here because of your dad and to get answers and…" Now was not the time to unload every last detail. They needed some peace. "I need you to know that I've stayed for you."

"Because you love me."

"Yes." She debated not responding but she couldn't hide this from him. She had fallen. Quickly and unexpectedly. Hard and against every defense she'd set up to keep him at a distance. What she felt for him was bigger than she thought possible and so scary because she still didn't know how much he could handle. Well, she did, but she didn't think he knew.

He shifted their position until he balanced on an elbow above her. "Then you should know that I made the offer for you to come here because I wanted you here. Because I found your attitude sexy. Every part of you sexy."

She tucked one of her hands between his side and the couch cushion. The other fell on the pillow by her head. "Oh, really?"

"Like this part." He unbuttoned the top of her dress. Opened each one so slowly, until he moved the sides away and unveiled her skin. He ran a finger over the top of her right breast, right where it plumped out over her bra. "And definitely this part." That finger traveled, sweeping over her breast and down toward the bit of bare stomach he'd revealed.

He lowered his head and licked his tongue over her bottom lip, taking it into his mouth before he kissed her. The touch lasted for a few seconds before he lifted up again. "Should we move—"

"No. Here." The kiss, so warm and inviting, had her breathless.

He glanced at the couch around them. "I like your style."

"And I'd like this better off." Her fingers went to work on his shirt and he raced to help her. In a few minutes they had it off and then it fell to the floor. The T under it followed.

Then his hand slipped under the edge of her skirt. It was the type that hung full and swingy but it had caught on her upper thigh. He pushed it even higher.

"Your skin is so soft." His thumb trailed up her inner thigh, right to the junction between her legs. "Next time you can skip the underwear."

"At a family dinner?" She managed to get the question out over the sensations bombarding her. That thumb rubbed over her, tracing circles on her underwear, over her heat.

"Is that weird?"

She wanted to punch him for sounding so in control. "A little, but I like weird."

"Do you like this?" One of his fingers slipped under the elastic band of her underwear. Slid over her bare skin, then inside her.

She grabbed onto his shoulder. "Carter."

"I'll take that as a yes." He bent down again and kissed her through her bra.

The combination of touching and kissing sent her temperature spiking. The need to rip off the rest of her clothes swamped her. She didn't want anything between them except the one thing they needed.

"Any chance you brought more condoms?"

He lifted his head just long enough to answer. "I left some in the nightstand drawer a while ago."

His finger pressed in and out of her in time with the sweep of his tongue. A few more minutes of this and she wouldn't be able to move. She struggled to keep her mind focused. "Go get one and I'll show you."

She had no idea how she was going to walk. "Me?"

"I want to watch you." He leaned back, giving her enough room to slide out from under him.

If he wanted to play, they could play. But she did not intend to be the only one losing control. Being breathless and needy was a two-person game. That's why she didn't waste any time. She grabbed two condoms and returned to the living room. Took her sweet time walking back to him, swaying her hips. Letting the front of her dress fall open just a bit more.

His gaze never left her. He shifted around on the couch until he lay on his back. Took his time looking up and down, inspecting every inch of her with that sly smile on his face.

She hitched up the skirt of her dress and kneeled on the floor beside the couch. He watched in silence as she unbuckled his belt and lowered his zipper. His breathing grew faster. This close, she could see the labored rise and fall of his chest as she ran her fingers over the front of his briefs.

"Hanna." He made her name sound like a plea.

His breath hitched when she slipped the material off him, freeing him. Then she lowered her head. Her tongue swirled over his tip as her hand pumped up and down. She licked him, squeezed him, brought him into her mouth. She kept it up when his fingers curled into her hair and his hips arched off the couch.

"Hanna, now."

He was begging. She could hear it in his voice and she lifted her head to see his face. The color had returned. His mouth dropped open and he fought for breath. She could feel the slight tremble in his muscles.

Having the ability to snap his control and give him so much pleasure made her feel powerful. Sexy.

"So bossy," she teased.

Ready now, she stood up and slipped off her underwear. Shimmied her hips, putting on a little show for him as he raced to get the condom on. Wedging one leg into the couch cushions, she straddled his hips but she wasn't quite ready to put him out of his misery. She bent her head and dragged her tongue up his chest. Let her hair brush over his bare skin.

She heard his hiccup of breath and felt his hands squeeze her hips and knew it was time. Lowering her body down ever so slowly, she slid over him. Those tiny inner muscles protested at first, then tightened around him. He filled her as she pressed down, making her fight to pull in enough air to breathe.

She felt full and hot and ready. And when she started to move, pleasure crashed over her. She controlled every plunge. He guided her body over his, but he let her take the lead. Her hands balanced on his chest and her fingernails curled into his skin. If he minded the tiny bites, he didn't show it. He was too busy panting.

A sheen of sweat appeared on his forehead as he held back, adjusting to her rhythm. It didn't take her long to feel the pull inside her. A few well-placed touches from him and her body had been primed and ready. The stretching sensation, the way she could move until he hit just the right spot, it all had her tumbling over the edge.

The orgasm ripped through her before she could slow it down. Her hips shifted forward and her head fell back. She felt hot and sensitive and when the pulses started she rode them out, grinding her body against his. She bit back a smile when he groaned.

The next few minutes were a blur of sensation. She felt him move under her and those hands tighten against her. His legs tensed and his back rose off the

bed. By the time they were done, they lay in a panting heap on the couch. Her hair swept over him and
his hand rubbed up and down her back.

She blinked and the room came into view. It took
a few more seconds for her voice to return. "For the
record, I love this position."

"Consider me a fan."

His laugh rumbled through her. Every part of her
that touched him, which was most of her, shifted as
his chest moved. She loved being this close, feeling
what he felt. "We should probably get up."

"Later." He kissed her forehead. "Much later."

She dreaded later. That's when she would have to
tell him the rest.

Twelve

Carter almost dreaded seeing Spence and Jackson pull up the long drive to the estate the next morning. So much for the idea of alone time with Hanna. He watched from the library window as they got out of the black sedan and walked up to the front door, shaking their heads and talking.

He could tell from their expressions, this was not going to be good.

Hanna looked up from her seat at his desk where they had been having coffee and enjoying the slow morning while he talked with her about his idea for the estate. The one only Jackson knew. "What's wrong?"

Funny how she knew there was a problem just by looking at him. Carter couldn't remember anyone ever being able to read him that well. She had said she loved him and he believed her. He toyed with the idea of saying it back but once he did that was it. There would be no room for him to maneuver, and he wasn't sure he was ready for that. Not when he sensed she still kept something big from him.

"We have company," he said, trying to take his mind off her and how right it felt to have her in his space and prepare for whatever was about to happen.

Putting aside the rough draft of the plans he'd been writing to restructure the estate, she frowned. "Is that a bad thing?"

He almost laughed because a few days ago she would have balked at the idea of anyone stopping by. She also wouldn't have been sitting with him, helping him work, being a sounding board for the ideas he intended to bring to Spence and Derrick for consideration. "In this case, I think so."

It took a few more minutes for Spence and Jackson to join them. They walked in, nodding a welcome to Hanna but not making a smart comment about her being there. That, alone, was unlike them.

Spence wore an unreadable expression as he leaned against one of the many bookcases outlining the room. "I have some bad news."

Carter had barely recovered from the last news he received. He wasn't sure he ever would. It had been one day. One very long day. "More?"

"I know you're still reeling from…" Spence's gaze shot to Hanna, then back to Carter. "You know."

Jackson rolled his eyes. "Subtle."

Hanna must have thought so, too. She closed the folder in front of her and untucked the leg she was sitting on. "I was there, Spence. You don't have to tread carefully."

But Spence was already shaking his head. "Don't be so sure."

"Okay." That was enough for Carter. "What's going on?"

"Dad is coming to town. Like, now." Spence focused on Carter. "He's on the way."

Carter's mind refused to grasp the concept. "Excuse me?"

"What?" Hanna practically screamed her response.

Jackson sighed as he sat down on the chair in front of Hanna. "Her tone sounded more appropriate under the circumstances."

The unexpected news also happened to be unwelcome. Carter had figured he'd have more time before his father blew back into town. The man couldn't even enjoy the beach the right way.

Carter didn't move from the window as he stared at his brother. "Talk."

"So yesterday, after dinner..." Spence winced as he glanced at Jackson. "Wanna help me out here?"

Jackson shook his head. "Not really."

This wasn't an easy topic. They all hated the idea of more time with Dad. Carter got that, but still. He needed to know what they were dealing with here. "Spence."

"I was furious on your behalf." Spence looked at Hanna. "Not at you. At the idea of Dad threatening you and your sister, possibly—"

"She gets it." Carter did not want to rehash the story again.

Spence nodded. "Anyway, the idea that he bribed you—"

"Tried to," Hanna said, breaking in to Spence's story before he could even get started.

They all stared at her. Only Jackson said what the other men were thinking. "Meaning what exactly?"

"I didn't take the money."

Jackson snorted. "Why not?"

"Good question," Spence said right after.

Her mouth dropped open as her gaze moved around the room. Whatever she saw had her scowling. "You all think I should have grabbed the hush money?"

That one was easy. Carter didn't have to think about it. "Yes."

"And ran. Fast and far." Jackson shook his head. "Honestly, I'm still confused that this is a question."

"The man has plenty. He deserves to lose some," Spence pointed out.

The men-are-idiots look on her face suggested she disagreed. "We all know it would have backfired on me. He could have made up anything. Said I blackmailed him. No way was I taking that risk."

"Let's get back to the reason we're here." Jackson leaned back in the fragile antique chair, ignoring the groaning of the wood beneath him. "And I'm happy to see you guys seem to have made up, by the way."

Spence glared at Jackson. "Really? You lectured me about their privacy the whole way here."

Jackson shrugged. "I'm not problematic like you are."

"Gentlemen." Hanna's voice managed to rise above the arguing. "Say what you came to say."

"I got ticked off and called Dad. Completely unloaded on him. Might have pointed out that none of us trust him." Spence rushed through the explanation, then stopped.

Silence settled in the library. For a few seconds, the only sound came from the ticking of the grandfather clock in the corner. Carter didn't realize how loud it was until just then.

"Did you specifically reference me and Gena?" Hanna asked.

Spence didn't avoid eye contact. "I called him about what happened with both of you, Hanna."

Hanna shot Spence a murderous look.

"Spence's interference came from a good place." Jackson's smile faltered when Hanna turned her focus to him. "Oh."

She just sat there, not saying anything. Carter didn't know how to make this better. He couldn't exactly blame his brother for doing what he had debated doing all night. At one point, he'd slipped out of the bed, forced himself to leave Hanna's side and picked up his cell. He'd toyed with the idea of calling Tortola but stopped when he heard Hanna moving around beneath the covers.

Her breathing seemed to slow now as she blew out a long breath. "So, your father knows I'm here."

Spence nodded. "Yes."

"And now he's coming."

Spence looked a little less sure. "Still yes."

She shook her head. "I can't see him."

"He's going to see me." This was a fight Carter

intended to have the minute his father showed up. Eldrick could disown him again for all Carter cared.

Spence nodded. "All of us. He should expect a wall of anger when he lands."

"You're going to challenge him?" Hanna asked in a voice that was less stern than a second ago.

"Derrick suggested we insist Dad sign over the company and go away or we start talking in public." Spence smiled but it quickly faded when he looked at Hanna. "Not about you. About all the other things he's done."

She dropped her head in her hands. Carter had no idea how to read that or guess what reaction would come next.

When she lifted her head again, some of the fight had run out of her. She looked tired. Maybe still a bit annoyed. "You can't...he's your father. There's probably some business agreement in place. Confidentiality or something. That seems like a thing rich people would do."

Jackson made a humming sound. "Right? So paranoid."

"Carter, I don't want to come between—"

"Do not finish that sentence." Now his anger rose to meet hers. He refused to go another round of them competing to see who felt guiltier. Enough of that. "The man scared a pregnant woman. He hid the reality of my own kid from me. And he tried to bribe you. He scared you. Enough that you moved to New York. That you had to beg to get your deceased father's property back."

She clenched her hands together in front of her. "He's a terrible man and apparently an appalling father. I'm not denying that."

"Which is why I called and yelled at him."

She turned on Spence. Pointed right at him. "You're not forgiven yet."

"Hey." Carter moved forward then. He stood in front of her with his hands resting on the edge of the desk. "You don't have to be there, Hanna, but we need to draw the line. If there's more, we need to know it. He needs to come clean."

Her shoulders fell. "I'm sorry."

"For what?"

She bit her bottom lip. She looked like she was about to say something then shook her head. It took another few seconds for her to speak. "That you're related to him. That he's caused so much damage. I don't know. For everything?"

"Well, that all ends now. We're going to confront him and let him know we're tired of him playing games and pretending to be in charge."

"You could lose everything." Her voice had a pleading quality to it.

But on this point, she didn't need to feel any guilt. He smiled at her. "Not possible."

"The house and trust funds are out of his control," Spence said.

For a second the news didn't seem to settle. Then her eyes widened. "How did he let that happen?"

"He's actually a terrible businessman." Jackson leaned back a bit too far in the chair. A cracking sound had him jerking forward again. "His schemes worked back when things were done by a handshake. He couldn't function in the modern world. Derrick is the brains behind the operation."

Spence smiled. "And, the reality is, he couldn't screw everyone."

She still looked confused. Not that anyone could blame her. "What does that mean?"

Carter loved this part. "He was trying to hide assets when he started playing around with the company accounts and got caught. The only way to hide them was to move some items to our mom's name. He thought they had an agreement to switch things back. He believed she trusted him, but she was smarter than he gave her credit for. She put almost everything in our names instead."

"He doesn't own this estate anymore and while he can take most of the money away and shut down or sell the business as majority stakeholder, he can't take what we already got from Mom," Spence explained.

"And what's left over from her is more than most people will see in a lifetime." Jackson held up a hand as if to apologize for jumping into the middle of the talk. "Just saying."

She looked at all of them one more time. "You'll be out of a job. You all will."

Jackson made a noise that sounded like *nah*. "I'll be fine."

"You guys sound so sure." But hope lingered in her voice. It was tough to miss the sound.

Carter got it. In some ways, Eldrick seemed untouchable. Even Derrick had covered for some of the schemes a few years ago so the company could be rebuilt. "After a lifetime of dealing with his garbage, we are sure of this one thing. It needs to be over."

Spence nodded. "Trust us."

It took a few more seconds but she finally smiled. "I do."

The sun felt good on her face as she stood by the fence on the state lawn.

Hanna counted back, thinking about the overcast days and the rain. She hadn't been outside for more than a walk between buildings or in and out of the car in three days. This morning, the sun streamed over the lawn, highlighting the bright red and orange of the leaves on the ground.

Fall would settle in soon. Under her original plan she would have been gone already, but she had no intention of moving on. Not yet. Carter hadn't formally asked her to stay or really even responded to her admission of being in love with him, not with words anyway. But he'd made it clear he wanted her around.

For now, that was good enough. The days with him, the nights… She wouldn't trade those for anything.

She let her head drop back and her hair fall down her shoulders. Closing her eyes, she soaked in the layer of warmth just above the cool breeze.

"We had a deal."

His voice. It snapped her out of her good mood. Out of everything.

She turned to see Eldrick Jameson standing in front of her. He was in his sixties and handsome, though she didn't see it. Other people mentioned it. He had a regal air about him, like he'd just stepped out of a country club magazine. Today he wore a navy blazer. She actually looked for a crest because he seemed like a guy who would have one of those.

If life were fair, he'd be ugly and have fangs, but no. He still had a trim figure with his salt-and-pepper gray hair. He'd aged well, which blew apart all those sayings about living hard…and karma.

"You're here." Like in every nightmare she'd had since he'd tried to bribe her.

He crossed his arms in front of him. "It's my house."

A strange lightness filled her. She almost smiled. "That's not what I heard."

"That trust?" He shook his head. "I can break that."

He sounded so sure. It was as if the rules didn't apply to him. From the stories she heard and what she read in her father's journal, they kind of didn't.

She wasn't the type who wanted to be rescued by a man, but the idea of having reinforcements right now sounded good. "Carter is—"

"Weak."

Eldrick hadn't seen him yet, but Carter walked across the lawn now with a woman beside him. Hanna knew she should whisper or at least change the topic because Carter deserved better, but she couldn't let that comment slide.

"What is wrong with you?" What kind of man spoke about his children that way? She didn't get it.

The footsteps stopped and Carter sighed as he waited behind his father. "I've been wondering that for years."

Before Eldrick could respond, the woman stepped forward. Hanna had a hard time with ages but she looked way younger than Eldrick, but not nearly as young as Hanna expected his fourth wife to be. With her billowy wide-legged pants, slim sweater jacket and shoulder-length auburn hair, she looked maybe forty, and carefree. Like she belonged on an island. The fake smile plastered on her face suggested she'd prefer to be there right now.

"You said you were going into the office."

The woman didn't have an accent. Her expensive clothes and the sparkly diamond rings she wore on most of her fingers spoke for her.

"Soon, my love." Eldrick had the nerve to sound sweet, maybe even a little charming.

Hanna hated that.

Carter stared at his father. "She called me to ask where you were. I told her you weren't really welcome at the office."

Hanna loved hearing the strength in Carter's voice. She'd never seen him back down and he wasn't doing it with his father either. For the first time she felt like she had support. That Carter would back her. That he really would fight for her. That security, that sense of being believed and protected gave her the mental push she needed. She'd tell him the rest and somehow it would all be okay.

But they had to get through this messy confrontation first.

"I own the business. I built it and—"

Carter held up a hand, seemingly not caring that he was taking on his father. "Enough with that."

"Do not interrupt me." There was an angry edge to Eldrick's voice now. That smarmy smile disappeared, revealing the slimy guy underneath.

"I'm Beth." The other woman held her hand out to Hanna.

"Technically, she's Jacqueline Annabeth Winslow Jameson," Carter added.

The smile Beth sent Carter looked genuine, even affectionate, as if she actually considered him family. "I go by Beth."

Hanna was still trying to recover from that name. It was quite a mouthful. "Why the nickname?"

Beth gave Hanna's hand a firm shake. "Eldrick isn't fond of the name Jacqueline."

A memory screeched to a halt in Hanna's head. Those journal entries about women Eldrick had slept with. About her father's conclusions.

The biggest one centered on the name Jack.

Eldrick broke through her mental gymnastics with his stern voice. "You and I need to have a talk about the rumors you're spreading."

There was no way Hanna would cower or run off. She might have given him the satisfaction last time. Not now. "You know what you did."

Beth took a step forward to stand by Hanna's side. "What?"

"It's nothing, Beth." Eldrick reached for his wife.

She waved him off, keeping her attention on Hanna. "Is it nothing?"

Hanna was torn between spilling the whole tale and trying to figure out which side this woman was on. She sounded so sincere and concerned, but Hanna had been reeled in by fake people before. It was one of the reasons she was so careful now.

"I'll let you decide."

Eldrick pointed at her. "Don't say another word."

Carter moved until he was beside Hanna, with his body inches ahead of hers as if he were ready to throw up a shield, if needed. "Do not get in her face. Ever."

After a nod from Carter, Hanna got to the spilling part. "He bribed me not to tell Carter that my sister had been pregnant with Carter's baby when she died."

Beth's eyes widened and her hand went to Hanna's arm. "Died? I'm so sorry."

"She killed herself after Dad threatened her," Carter said, not backing down either.

"That is not what happened." This time Eldrick grabbed his wife's hand and pulled her over to stand with him. "I told you these boys exaggerate. Ignore him."

Beth looked at Carter. "When?"

He didn't pretend to be confused. Didn't hesitate. "About six months ago."

"After we were married."

"Now, Beth." Eldrick patted his wife's arm while he scowled at Hanna. "Why are you even here?" Then he switched to Carter. "Don't you get it? This woman's goal is to cause trouble. She burst in here, making these claims."

Carter shook his head. "I went to see her as part of *your* requirements."

"What does that mean?" Beth asked.

Eldrick tried to answer, but Carter talked over him. "The things my brothers and I have to do before he'll consider turning the everyday operations over to Derrick. Each brother got an assignment. Finding Hanna and handing her an envelope was mine."

"I bet you cashed that check."

Now it made sense. The envelope was Eldrick's last effort to pay her off. He likely thought sending Carter would intimidate her in some way. The man did not know his son at all.

"This is all so confusing. Check?" Beth rubbed her forehead as she looked at Carter. "And Derrick already runs the business."

A stiff wind blew over the lawn. Hanna shivered but she thought it might be a reaction to the confidence pulsing off Carter rather than the cold. He looked so sure, so in control. So perfect…for her. No wonder she loved him.

Carter continued, "Eldrick needs to officially retire and step out or he can come back anytime."

Beth turned on her husband. "That's not what you told me."

"We're talking about Ms. Wilde right now."

Eldrick's tone was so soft.

Such garbage. "So condescending."

The sound of Hanna's voice seemed to tick Eldrick off. This time he went after Carter. "This was all your fault. You weren't careful. Dropping your pants and not using protection. What kind of man are you?"

"A real one who doesn't threaten women." Carter's voice stayed even. He never lost control. Standing tall and sure, he looked ready to take on any battle.

Eldrick shook his head as he continued to spew. "You made the mess and, as usual, I had to clean it up."

Anger lit up the inside of Hanna's head until she thought it might explode. "Gena was not a mess."

"I did you a favor," Eldrick said, still talking to Carter.

"Eldrick, the woman is dead." Beth's voice was sharp and biting now. Whatever tolerance she'd had, it vanished.

"Which is a shame but not my fault, and I don't appreciate the suggestion otherwise." Eldrick kept talking at Carter, who stood there looking bored, as if the words bounced off him. "You never learn your lesson. I got you out of one entanglement and then you shack up with the other sister?"

Hanna didn't know how Carter could stand to listen to the man. She sure couldn't. "Gena wasn't an entanglement either."

"I think it's time you leave the property." Eldrick pointed in the general direction of the street. "Whatever you're searching for, you're not going to find it here. You have your check. Now run along."

When that didn't work he took a step forward, reaching for her. Carter blocked the move. He stood right in front of her.

"She is with me. You aren't to go near her again." This time Carter's voice seethed with anger.

Eldrick tried to look around his son's impressive shoulders at Hanna. "He's ungrateful. And unemployed. Did he tell you that? Never held a real job. Never contributed."

It was now or never. Eldrick's usual hold on the conversation faltered. The concern on Beth's face was tough to miss. Carter looked ready to go into battle for her. But this Hanna needed to do.

She stepped around Carter, facing Eldrick head-on. "How did my father really die?"

The question seemed to flatten him. He took a step back as his eyes darted to the side. "What?"

She didn't hold back. "We both know he didn't fall off a ladder. The man built houses. He wasn't sloppy."

"He made a mistake and paid a steep price."

She felt a hand on her lower back. She knew it was Carter and it meant he supported her. He didn't even need to say the words to get her to keep going. "Taking a job from you, yes. But you didn't answer my question."

Beth shook her head. "I don't understand."

"He worked for us and died on the job. That's all I know. You've seen the reports. You know the truth. It was an unfortunate workplace accident," he said, showing he knew far more than he pretended to now. "Your mother already tried for a bigger payday and failed."

He could launch any accusation he wanted. Hanna intended to stand there and take it. "Did you push him?"

"Of course not." Eldrick looked over her head at Carter. "Usher her off the grounds or I will."

"What did you do, Dad?" Carter asked.

"Nothing. The lawyers already—"

"Eldrick?" Beth put her hand on his arm and looked up at him. "Just say it."

At the sound of her voice, Eldrick's resolve seemed to crumble. He didn't stand quite as tall and his words sputtered a bit as he spoke. "This has been resolved."

Beth's perfectly manicured eyebrow lifted. "Apparently not."

"This is your last chance." Carter's hand flattened on Hanna's back. He wasn't doing anything to hide the fact they were together and she had his support. "You answer her or I'll open an investigation. We'll go through every report and all the findings. Bring in people who worked here. Do re-creations if we need to. Blow this wide and make it public."

Hanna loved him for who he was and she loved him for those words. It was a promise to her as much as a threat against his father.

"It's not anything," Eldrick said.

Carter swore under his breath. "The man is dead."

"Fine." Eldrick brushed a hand down the front of his blazer. "There was a piece of equipment. It malfunctioned. End of story."

Hanna had been holding her breath and now it rushed out of her. The knot in her stomach that had been there since the day her father died eased. For a second, she could breathe without being hit with the weight of unfinished business. "I knew it."

"He was working on it and there was a burst of hot air that blew him off." Eldrick waved his hand in the air as if the conversation were done. "That's it."

"Why not tell the truth back then?" she asked. The secrecy only created more doubt.

"It was an accident."

But not the same accident she'd heard all her life. "One your machinery caused."

"He fudged the story because it would have cost him otherwise." Carter sounded tired and frustrated and two seconds from losing his control. "Right? You knew the machine was a problem. Maybe Hanna's dad warned you, and you didn't bother to get it fixed."

Beth tugged on Eldrick's arm. "You put that man in a position to be hurt?"

"That's not what happened."

But it was. Hanna understood now.

This was about liability. Whatever feelings he'd had for her father, and she doubted Eldrick had many since he only cared about himself and maybe a little about Beth, those feelings didn't outweigh the fact that her father's death was a nuisance to him.

The realization made her want to scream and pound on his chest. That he could forfeit a life because it was cheaper than fixing equipment. Her mind couldn't grasp that at all. She leaned into Carter's side because she wasn't sure her legs would hold her much longer.

"We're leaving." Beth dropped her hand from Eldrick's arm. Nothing about her tone suggested she wanted to hear an argument.

Of course, Eldrick tried anyway. "I need—"

"To come with me right now." Beth started walking.

Carter shook his head. "I'd listen to her."

"I'll be back." Eldrick waited until his wife's back was turned to glare at Hanna again. "You need to be gone."

Carter slipped an arm around her. Put it on her shoulder and pulled her in even closer to his side. "She's staying."

"Don't fight me on this, Carter."

"From now on, expect a fight on everything."

Eldrick hesitated before walking away. In a few long strides, he caught up with Beth. They headed along the side of the house without saying a word.

Hanna expected to hate Eldrick's newest wife. She'd pictured one type of woman, a sort of female version of Eldrick. Once again, her preconceived notions had been wrong.

"So, your stepmom…"

"She's turned out to be a surprise. Most of the women he married went along with his schemes, at least in front of us. They all left shortly after finding out some new horrible thing he did in the past. She's sticking around, holding him accountable."

Hanna broached the one open question. "The name thing?"

Carter scoffed. "That's odd even for my dad. What kind of man makes a woman use a different name?"

"Do you think it means something?" Because Hanna did. She thought it was about Eldrick and his secrets. She wished she could be sure because once she exposed this last one she would turn all of their lives upside down. Before she took that step and launched one more emotional grenade at Carter, she'd think it through.

Carter shrugged. "My father has to control everything."

"Not anymore."

This time Carter laughed. "No, not anymore."

Thirteen

Later that night, Carter sprawled on the couch in the television room with Hanna leaning on his chest. By silent agreement they had started spending their nights in the main house. He'd insisted the furniture was more comfortable and she just rolled her eyes and went along with the excuse.

Today had been long and trying. Finding out his father had contributed to her father's death had not been an easy afternoon. Carter was starting to wonder if he'd ever have an easy one again. But this part he enjoyed, having her back rest against his chest. Listening to her laugh at some dumb joke in this lame buddy heist movie.

Somehow, she'd eased the harsh news into the rest of the day. After an hour of being alone, walking the grounds while he watched helpless and in desperation from the window, she'd bounced back. It was as if hearing the news had freed her to move on.

That made one of them. It knocked him down. He mentally struggled to understand why she didn't pack her bag and run as far away from the Jamesons as possible.

He slipped his fingers through her hair. "I love that you're here with me. Despite all the bad memories, this house has always been special to me. With you it's even more so."

"Sweet talker."

But he didn't want her to think it was a line. He'd never expected her to love him. It was a gift. And with each day his feelings for her became clearer. She'd been so unexpected that he was still trying to get his emotional footing. She deserved more and not just when it came to them.

"I feel like I should apologize for everything that happened to your family." He kissed the side of her hair, inhaling the scent of her floral shampoo. "I don't even know where to start."

She shifted, turning to look up at him. "I kept the baby information from you."

"Do you know if it was a boy or a girl?" He hadn't meant to ask that. He wasn't even sure where the question came from since he'd been blocking out any thoughts of the baby all day.

She slipped her hand over his knee. "A little girl."

An image flashed in his mind and he pushed it out again. "Was she healthy?"

"Yes." Hanna flipped around. Her legs balanced over his as she sat sideways, facing him. "I can't explain what happened that day. What one thing pushed her over the edge. I wish I could."

"Me, too."

She leaned her head against the back cushion of the couch. "The doctors I talked to explained that it's like darkness. Not just a lack of light. It's more like a weight and it shoves you down and spins tales in your head and convinces you there is no way out. Nothing, not sunshine or trying to be happy or any of the other things people talk about as possible ways through it really work. The darkness is relentless, joyless. It presses and presses until you break."

He brushed a hand over her hair. The silky strands slipped through his fingers. "Have you ever experienced it?"

"I used to think depression equaled extreme sadness, but now I know that's wrong. It's a much bigger, soul-sucking thing." She slid her fingers through his and brought their joined hands to her mouth.

"Is it weird for you that we're together after I spent that weekend with her?" He had been avoiding that question from the start. For him, the sisters were so different that he didn't even connect them in his mind.

"I try not to think about that part."

"I don't compare you." He stressed each word because he needed her to believe him. "You're distinctly Hanna. Not a substitute. Not the 'other' sister. Just Hanna."

She kissed the back of his hand. "Thank you."

"You knew that, right?"

"I think I needed to hear it since I'd spent so much of my life in my sister's shadow."

There was more. Feelings he hadn't expected. New priorities he'd tried to ignore but they refused to be pushed aside. "I'm not a guy who sticks around and fights through things."

She smiled. "I've heard."

"From?"

"You." She dropped their joined hands to her lap. "You've been pretty honest that settling in is not your thing."

Not before. Now he wasn't so sure.

He looked at the long stretch of life in front of him and he no longer saw travel and moving and switching houses and being alone. He thought about his brothers and the estate. About her.

Maybe this was how it happened. He'd made fun of his brothers for falling so fast. For acting like they'd lost all sense. He kind of understood it now.

"I think putting down roots could be the new me."

When she didn't laugh or run out of the room, he kept going. "The idea of making the estate into something new, an event space, a place for parties. Something other than a home. A place that employs lots of people and offers opportunities. That sounds good to me."

"And you would run it."

"Yeah. I'd build it and expand it and live here." But when he envisioned the plans, he saw her. Them eating dinner and lounging around like they were doing now. "You still married to the idea of living in New York?"

She lifted her head just long enough to tuck her hair behind her ear. "Why, do you need someone to clean this place?"

He laughed. "Yeah, a team of people, but what I'm really saying is I don't want you to go."

Her fingers tightened on his. "That's a big statement."

The biggest, because what he was really saying was he wanted her here, for a long time. Forever.

"What I feel for you is big." They sounded so serious as they sat there whispering. He couldn't help but lighten the mood. "Admittedly, maybe not preteen crush big."

"Ugh." She buried her face in her hands. "You knew about that?"

The embarrassment and mumbling were endearing. She could be hot and sexy and sweet and charming. The combination blew his control to pieces.

"The teen me might have ignored you. The grown-up me is so much smarter."

She lifted her head and started frowning. "What is that sound?"

The buzzing didn't let up. Carter reached for the remote and clicked on the number to show the security feed. "The box at the entry gate out front."

"Isn't that fancy?" Then she leaned forward to study the screen. "Wait, is that your stepmom?"

The image didn't lie. Beth stood there, without Eldrick or anything but a purse and stared at the house. "That can't be good."

"At least she's alone."

Carter lifted Hanna's legs off his lap and stood up. "That's what I mean. We're all doomed if she left him."

"Why do you say that?"

"She's the reason he lives in Tortola."

* * *

He went downstairs to retrieve Beth and ushered her into the television room about ten minutes later. Her usual put-together style seemed to be failing. A lock of her hair fell across her forehead and she kept playing with the metal band of her very expensive watch.

She stepped into the room, saw Hanna and the last of her blank expression fell. Beth's attitude morphed from *I'm fine* to *I'm barely holding it together* in a few seconds. "I'm sorry to disturb you."

"Come inside." Hanna stood up and gestured for Beth to sit on the couch. "Are you okay?"

"She left my Dad."

Carter knew because he heard the terrible news on the walk up the stairs. He nearly tripped in response. He could hardly wait to hear Jackson's and his brothers' reactions when he sent them a group text.

"Oh." Hanna shot him a grimace over the top of Beth's head as she helped the older woman sit down. Not that Beth needed an assist but her hands did shake and Hanna seemed concerned.

The watchband clasp snapped as Beth opened and closed it. "He lied about everything."

"It's what he does."

Hanna shot Carter a look that said he should be quiet. He just shrugged in return.

Beth didn't appear to hear him anyway. She sat there, shaking her head as she stared at her lap. "All those promises that he was a new man. How loving me changed things."

"I actually think it did." That got her attention. Carter didn't say the words just to comfort her. He really did mean them. "The father I grew up with would never step away from the business, even temporarily, and move to an island to make someone else happy. You mean something to him."

"How am I supposed to trust him?"

He had to look at Hanna because the pleading in Beth's eyes proved to be too much after today's events. "You've got me there."

"Carter." Hanna stared at the empty space on the other side of Beth on the couch. "Sit down."

That much closeness struck him as unnecessary. He doubted Beth wanted his company but Hanna's glare didn't exactly give him a choice.

"I just wasn't sure where to go. We were here this afternoon, so I remembered this address."

"It's fine." Carter wasn't sure what else to say, so he went with that.

"Do you have a bag?" Hanna asked.

Carter did not like where this was going. He could sense his world turning upside down. Again.

Beth shook her head. "I left it at the condo."

"What condo?"

"Dad kept a place here," Carter said, answering Hanna's question.

"You rich guys have a thing for property."

Leave it to Hanna to take a second out of consoling to land a shot. "Is now the time?"

"You should stay here," Hanna said, ignoring him. "I'm sure we can find you what you need. I don't have much, but I'm happy to share."

Beth smiled at Hanna. "You're very sweet."

Carter still hadn't recovered from that move when Hanna shot him a do-something look over the top of Beth's head. He knew he'd get sucked into this. "Make a list and I'll go grab what you need."

Beth shrugged. "A new husband."

"That may take me more than fifteen minutes." Carter jumped up and looked around for his phone. "I'll call Lynette to make up a room."

"Don't bother her. I'll do it."

Again with this. "Hanna, you don't work for me."

Beth put her hand on Hanna's knee. "I don't want to be in the way."

"There are a ridiculous number of bedrooms in this place. You can have one. Right, Carter?" Hanna looked up at Carter with an expression that suggested he better get the answer correct.

"Sure." Who wouldn't want the stepmother he barely knew to stay over when she was fighting with the father he hated? "Top of the stairs, first door on the right. It's a guest suite and all yours."

Beth nodded. "Just for tonight."

Carter doubted that would be true. "For as long as you need it."

He felt obligated to say that as he watched her leave the room and head for the hall. He waited until she disappeared to turn back to Hanna.

"Now what?" she asked.

They should relocate to another state. Somewhere like Utah. That was the only option here, though Carter knew Hanna would say no. That left him without a Plan B for dealing with his father's inevitable return.

"I have no idea."

Fourteen

So much yelling.

Not at each other, just in general. Those thoughts kept moving through Hanna's mind as she listened to the brothers and Jackson argue about what to do about their father. He demanded to see his wife and was coming over to make that happen. Hanna sent out an emergency call and Ellie swooped in and grabbed Beth to prevent the confrontation.

That left only the men and Hanna at the estate. Even the people who worked there had scattered. As she watched Derrick pace from one side of the library to the other, she wondered if she should have headed out with Ellie and Beth. Carter had told her to go so she could avoid another meeting with his dad. The offer had been tempting but a voice in her head nagged at her to stay.

He couldn't hurt her anymore. That was a fact. Eldrick no longer scared her. He blustered and threatened and probably could make her life miserable, but she felt like part of a united front now. Everyone in this room, plus the women who weren't here, had committed to standing up to Eldrick and his manipulations. She'd turned down not one but two checks. He had no hold over her.

But he did have a hold on Carter.

He'd never admit it, but hearing his father discount him had to hurt. He might be an adult now, but the words, the constant barrage that continued even now, the loss of faith, that had to bash a person's self-esteem. She vowed not to let Eldrick take one more slice out of Carter. She loved Carter and her mind had started spinning with ideas about a future with him. That meant she did not want Carter near his father very often.

And then there was Jackson. She watched him now as he walked to the window, peeking out, trying to stay out of the fray. If she was right, he'd experienced the worst slight of all.

At ten after three, Hanna decided Eldrick wasn't coming. Maybe he'd figured out his sons had conspired against him. Worse, he might have gone looking for Beth. Not wanting to worry anyone with that thought, Hanna reached for her phone. Ellie and Derrick had security. She wanted to remind Ellie to use it.

"Where is she?" Eldrick's voice boomed through the room.

Hanna spun around, expecting him to look like a man on the verge of losing his wife. Nope. He wore an expensive blazer and polished shoes. If this was his version of heartbroken, she didn't see how it was any different from his usual entitled look.

"She's not here," Derrick said.

Eldrick barely gave his sons eye contact. "I'll go find her."

Spence stepped in front of him, blocking his path to the door. "We want to talk to you."

Eldrick's expression did not disappoint. His gaze swept across the room. "You will never get the business this way."

Carter shook his head. "This is about you."

"You should be at work," Eldrick said as he looked at Derrick. Never mind that it was Saturday. Then his gaze landed on her. "And you should be out of town. Somewhere with a mop in your hand."

She knew the words were calculated to hurt. Only in his world would pointing out what she did for a living be a slight.

"Stop talking." The order came from Carter.

"You think you can take me on, son?"

Carter shook his head. "I don't think you're worth it."

She loved that response. She almost cheered.

"I've had enough." Eldrick smiled as he looked at them. "I'll see you at work on Monday." He glanced at Derrick. "I'll expect you to vacate my office."

Rage swept through her as he issued threats. She thought about letting him walk out the door and then helping the men sift through the aftermath, but then she looked at Jackson. Looked at all of them. They deserved to know the truth.

She knew Carter believed all the secrets had been exposed. Dropping this one was a risk, but he needed to know the truth. Once he did she was confident he would help the others. And then, finally, there wouldn't be any more baggage left stacked between them. They'd have issues to handle but no secrets.

She stepped up next to the desk. "Tell them the truth."

Eldrick rolled his eyes. "Is this about your father again? I'm done talking about the accident."

She let that word slide right by her. She refused to be derailed. That's what he wanted. He thought he could land a few well-chosen words and send them all spiraling. He didn't know his audience. The Jameson men weren't like that and neither was she.

"It's about Jackson."

Jackson frowned. "Me?"

"I don't have to listen to you." But Eldrick no longer looked as smug.

That's when she knew she was right. All the connections she'd made in her head, all the pieces that were right there but everyone else had been too close to see.

"He deserves to know. They all do."

Carter appeared at her side. "What are you talking about?"

She had to ignore him and the confusion in his voice. Not look at his face. No, she needed to push through for Carter. Eldrick could not squirm his way out of this lie like he'd tried to with so many others.

"She's just like her sister." Eldrick glared at Carter. "When will you learn?"

"Hanna?" Derrick held up his hands as if hoping she would continue and explain.

"My father kept a journal."

Eldrick jumped right in, spoke almost before she finished her sentence. "A book of some man's fantasies. It's irrelevant."

He was unraveling. She could see him falling apart in front of her. "You know that's not what it was. He wrote about you. The things you said to him. Side comments. Details about your exploits."

That was the tame version. Apparently, Eldrick liked to brag. Her father wrote it all down, along with comments about how upsetting he found it because he really liked Carter's mother.

"That's man talk. Nothing more."

No way was she letting that stand as his excuse. "Tell him or I will."

"You don't know anything."

Jackson's gaze switched from Eldrick back to her. "What does this have to do with me?"

"Everything." She ached for him. Seeing Carter's confusion only made the moment worse.

She was about to take a wrecking ball to his world. But he had to know. They all did. Jackson had a birthright and a connection. Carter had more family, and she'd come to understand that as much as he might deny it, he was all about family. A man who returned to help his brothers was not disconnected, which only made her love him more.

"Shut up." Eldrick practically spit out the words as he took a few steps forward.

Carter blocked his path. "Don't talk to her like that."

"She is about to ruin everything."

Spence cleared his throat. "Then she better speak."

"You don't even know." Eldrick looked at Carter

and started to laugh. The evil sound filled the room. "That's rich. You're sleeping with her and she's sneaking behind your back, finding journals."

Carter didn't seem all that impressed with his father's act. But he did frown at her. "Hanna, tell me."

"No!" Some of Eldrick's calm faded then. He switched from laughing to explaining. The words rushed out of him. "I did this to protect you. Why do you think I sent you away? I couldn't let you date Zoe. She was off-limits."

There it was. Hanna closed her eyes, hoping to get hit by a wave of relief but all she felt was sadness. This man had actually disowned one of his kids to protect his secrets.

"How is my sister involved in this?" Jackson was standing up straight now, fully engaged.

"Zoe is your sister," Eldrick said to Carter. "Jackson is your brother." The words held all the emotion of a weather report. Purely factual, as if it were no big deal. "A mistake I made—"

"What?" All the color drained from Jackson's face.

"Your mother was a woman I knew. Worked in the office next door. It meant nothing, but you can't trust women when it comes to birth control. Not when we're dealing with this kind of money."

"Oh, my God." Spence's voice sounded small and stunned. "You think you're giving a fatherly lecture right now?"

"That's what I was doing with Gena. Making sure this didn't happen to you." Eldrick looked at Carter.

"Jackson and Zoe are our siblings." Carter said the words as if they'd just crystallized in his head.

"Half," Eldrick corrected.

Derrick scoffed. "As if that matters."

"Of course it does," Eldrick said. "They're not Jamesons. It's as simple as that."

He was unbelievable. He used words as a weapon and Hanna was sick of it. "Because of you. Because you made the decision not to tell."

Eldrick looked her up and down. "You're worse than that piece of trash sister of yours."

Carter lunged then, but Derrick caught him just in time. But that didn't stop Carter from staring at his father. "Get out."

"You can't order me to leave."

Carter shook his head. "Your name is not on the title to this house. You're not on the trust. You have no right to be here."

"Yeah, family only." Spence walked to the door and gestured for Eldrick to go.

"You're all going to regret this." But he didn't stay and say more.

His footsteps echoed on the elaborate staircase. No one said a word as the fighting continued to vibrate off the walls.

Hanna knew they couldn't take the risk of Eldrick getting to Beth or Ellie. "I'll call to warn—"

"You knew." Carter turned on her. "All of it."

A lump formed in her throat as she looked around. Saw the mix of pain, confusion and anger in their gazes. "I guessed."

"But you didn't tell me?"

Because she needed to be sure and they needed to have this conversation alone. She didn't plan to unload. She'd wanted to do this the right way, without

an audience. Not put Carter in a terrible position…
again. "It's not that simple."

"It is." He stepped closer. "You know how I feel
about Jackson. I might not have said that I considered
him family, but you could tell. You read people. We
talked about so many things."

Derrick winced. "Carter, maybe now isn't—"

"You didn't say anything. All those nights, all
that talking. You held back secret after secret. I for-
gave it all."

She didn't have to guess his mood now. There was
no pretending or trying to hide it. With every word
the fury built inside him and he aimed it right at her.
She didn't even try to duck.

"The journal didn't spell it out. I put it together
through Beth's real name and…there was this nota-
tion."

"When?" When she didn't immediately answer,
he continued his interrogation. "It's an easy question, Hanna. When?"

Part of her wanted to shrivel under the rapid-fire
questioning, but she forced her shoulders back. She
didn't do anything wrong. Another case of bad timing, maybe. But she was not the guilty party here.

"I found the journal right after I got here. When
Beth said her full name and how Eldrick hated her
real first name. It was a different spelling, but so
close to Jackson's." She said his name and turned to
him. "I'm sorry."

He just shook his head. "I don't get this."

Spence grabbed Carter's arm. "Stop and think
for a second."

She silently begged for Carter to listen. Eldrick

made the mess and she got stuck with the cleanup. She'd tried to stay away in the safety of New York. She'd put her teen crush behind her. She never expected to have her life tangled up with Carter's again. To ache to be with him. To love him until she couldn't think straight. "I know you're blaming me, but this was your dad. It's always about him."

"I don't expect anything from him, Hanna." Carter swallowed hard enough for her to see it. "I trusted you, or I tried to."

"Carter, please…"

But he just shook his head.

The tension in the room closed in on her. She tried to breathe but the suffocating pressure nearly choked her. She could feel Carter's anger, knew it was aimed at her. It pulsed off him and crashed right into her. She tried to hold on to her balance, to think of the right thing to say, but she could see he'd shut down. His mouth fell into a flat line and a coldness she'd never expected to see moved into his eyes.

She needed the cottage…no, she needed to go. He was the one who spent his life running and she got it now. Sometimes the crushing pain, the slip into the abyss as one more thing was lost, proved too much.

She rushed across the room, right past him. He didn't make a move to stop her, sending a slicing pain through her. It was Spence who touched her arm. "Don't leave."

"I can't stay."

Spence called out to his brother. "Carter, come on."

She didn't even need to see his face to know he'd given up on her. She'd betrayed him one time too many. Maybe it was a good thing he never told her he loved her. The weight of all she lost pummeled her, but at least she didn't lose his love.

She'd never had it.

Carter heard her go. Listened to her mumbling and knew his brothers were staring. Still, he couldn't move. He stood in the middle of the library, the one room in the house that gave him peace, and his world crumbled around him.

"That was a bloodbath." Derrick's voice sounded softer than usual. "Jackson?"

"I might throw up."

Carter looked at his friend, now brother. Jackson's shoulders curled in and he held on to the bookcase as if it were the only thing keeping him upright. "Don't blame you."

Jackson sat down hard in the desk chair. "I spend half of my day being grateful he's not my father, but he is."

"Did your mom ever give you any clue?" Spence asked.

Jackson shook his head. "None."

She'd died a few years ago. It seemed like she'd thought it was better her children never know. There was a part of Carter that understood that. Eldrick was a hard man, even to his children. "She was likely protecting you."

Carter rubbed his stomach. He tried to focus on the carnage in front of him, not let his mind wander to Hanna and the look on her face as she walked out.

"Zoe is going to lose it." Jackson looked up. His expression flipped from blank to concerned and back again. "Now you know why your dad pushed you away, disowned you. He was trying to keep you away from Zoe."

The logic made no sense to Carter. "Shows how much he knows about me. We were only ever friends."

"What were you thinking?" Jackson sounded confused now. "The way you unloaded on Hanna."

The words pounded into Carter. He had been expecting…well, anything else. "She lied to me."

Spence made a strangled sound. "How was she supposed to tell that story?"

"What if her theory had been wrong and she said it and caused a bigger mess?" Derrick asked.

Carter had no idea what was happening. They should be furious with her and with him for inviting her back into their lives.

"You guys are ganging up on me now?" He barely knew what to think and now he didn't have anywhere to turn.

"We tried to stop you a few minutes ago and that didn't work." Jackson pointed in Derrick's general direction. "Well, they did. I was too busy trying not to pass out or throw Eldrick out a window."

"You should have done the latter, but the former would have been funny." Spence actually laughed but then stopped when no one else made a sound. "But back to you."

For the first time in his life, Carter didn't know what to say. The speechless thing never happened to him, yet here he was. Stumped. "What?"

Spence shook his head. "You have to stop her."

What were they even talking about? "From?"

Jackson sighed. "If my guess is right, leaving."

"You didn't exactly support her." Derrick's look…
Was that disappointed?

Maybe they didn't understand. Carter decided to
try again. "She knew—"

Spence held up a finger. "Thought she knew."

That wasn't the point. Not the one he was trying
to make. "She didn't tell me."

Jackson frowned. "Since she was still dealing
with her sister's death and just learned that our father played a role in her father's death, maybe cut
her some slack."

"Look, I've been there." Derrick continued as if
he were telling a story. "You fall in love and become
vulnerable, then you say and do dumb things."

They'd all lost their minds. Yes, the news about
her father's death…maybe he wasn't taking that
enough into account. Carter felt a slap of guilt about
that. But the rest?

Jackson did his usual humming sound. "He's not
saying no to the love thing."

Love.

The word sat heavy on Carter's chest. He'd
thought about a life with her, but love still seemed
out of reach. "It's too early."

Both Spence and Derrick laughed but Derrick was
the one who responded. "Right. Because love works
that way. It has a time limit."

Spence took his turn. "You and Hanna have a lot
to talk about and work through but, personally, I'm
hoping you fix this."

"And stay." Derrick shrugged. "There, I said it."

"Carter has a business proposal for you guys concerning this estate," Jackson said.

The guy's world had been turned upside down and he managed to keep up with the conversation and offer insights. Carter had no idea how. He'd been shaken by the news he had more siblings and body slammed by the idea of being in love and spun up with anger about Hanna not talking to him…and now he wondered if his vulnerability on one front might have had something to do with his reaction to the other.

He could not find his footing at all.

"Good. If he fixes things with Hanna, we'll listen." Derrick ended the comment with a wink.

Carter was still reeling. But now that he'd had a moment to recover, he realized he'd made a misstep. His behavior hadn't risen to Eldrick levels, but he hadn't exactly been subtle or private in his condemnation. And he hadn't fought to keep Hanna here, with him. He'd made it so easy for her to leave him before he could leave her.

Thinking about all he needed to figure out and put back in order made his chest ache. "It's not that easy."

"Oh, it's not going to be easy." Derrick laughed at the thought. "But it will be worth it."

Jackson had gone quiet. He sat in the chair, looking into the distance.

"You okay?" Carter asked.

"No. It's unlikely I'll ever be okay again, but go."

Derrick nodded. "We'll babysit him."

Jackson let out what sounded like a groan. "Lucky me."

But there was one bright spot. Jackson might not see it, but Carter did. "We're family now."

The groan only grew louder.

Fifteen

Hanna stood over her duffel bag, knowing it was time. She'd opened it and thrown it on the bed. Next came the packing, and she had to do it. Despite all the flowery words and talk about her sticking around, she'd outstayed her welcome.

That scene at the house…

The information had needed to come out—for Carter, for Jackson, for everyone—but her delivery sucked. This seemed to be her thing. Have information and stumble into getting it to the people who needed it. She could still see their stunned expressions. The looks of shock and pain. And Carter's anger.

"Put the bag away unless you're packing to officially move in to the main house, which you need to do."

At the sound of Carter's voice, she turned around to find him lounging in the bedroom doorway. She'd seen that so many times over the last few weeks. He fit here. Always looked so comfortable in his skin, so sure.

But he'd told her that underneath it all he wasn't always so confident. The confession had sent her heart into a tailspin.

Looking at him now, it flipped right over.

That vulnerability and the way he expressed it softened her anger toward him. His words had been genuine. She was sure of that.

But right now, even though she loved him, she wanted to punch him.

"I'm leaving." She turned back to the bed. Her heartbeat raced and she quietly inhaled, trying to settle it down.

"No."

He walked around her and grabbed the duffel. "I can have Lynette or someone grab your stuff."

"What are you talking about?"

He hitched his finger in the direction of the living room. "Get that pretty butt of yours back up to the main house."

Pretty butt?

The ups and downs of being with him were killing her. "You've got to be kidding."

"I am done fighting with you, Hanna."

From the snap in his tone, she doubted that. Sounded like he had lots of fury he still needed to burn off. Well, no thank you.

"That would be nice."

He held up both hands as he walked across the

room to the end of the bed. "My reaction to the bomb you dropped wasn't great. I'm sorry for that. I'll do better, but you have to meet me partway."

His presence filled the room. Everywhere she looked held a memory of him. Now she had the live version staring her down. "Meaning?"

"You weren't completely honest with me, and I get to be pissed off about that." He sat on the end of the bed and watched her. "It won't last long. You'll probably say something funny in an hour or two and the edge will fade. I predict by tonight, I'll be fine."

"You'll be fine?" She repeated the words but they still didn't make sense to her.

What is happening?

Here she was, packing and halfway out the door, and he was talking about their usual movie night. It was as if the last hour hadn't happened.

He stared at her. "You have spent this entire relationship holding things back—"

"I didn't—"

"And I let you get away with that. I admit, I have to take part of the responsibility here. But enough. When you do stuff like this, I get to be angry. That's how relationships work."

This sounded like a lecture. He'd morphed from angry to professor. She refused to find that sexy. The in control thing…okay, that was a bit sexy. But still. "We are not in a relationship."

He rested his palms on the mattress and leaned back. "Since I'm in love with you, we sure as hell better be."

"What?" Her brain stopped working.

His words, that sly smile. With every minute, a bit more of the Carter she was used to came back to her.

"Yeah, it stunned me, too." He sat up straight again. "Do you know how much grief I'm going to take from my brothers after all the jokes I made about them being sad and pathetic? From all three of them. Wow... I am never going to get used to that."

In the confusion and with the touch of excitement at seeing him walking through the door, she forgot about Jackson. "How is he?"

"Floundering. Horrified to be related to us, which is understandable."

Giving up on the packing and trying to follow the conversation, she sat down next to him. If this was it, she needed to be clear about one thing. "I really didn't know."

He shot her one of *those* looks. "Don't engage in verbal gymnastics. You should have told me what you guessed and I think you know that."

She wanted to argue, but he wasn't exactly wrong. Not telling had felt safer. Everything had been going well and unloading one more thing on Carter had seemed like too much. "Would you have performed a secret DNA test?"

"Maybe." Then he reached for her. Snagged her around the waist and settled her on his lap. "This okay?"

She winced as she wrapped her arms around his neck and held on. She didn't want to let go.

Ten minutes ago, she'd felt hollow and empty and thought she'd never have this again, and she wasn't about to miss it this time. "I didn't want to hurt him."

"He knows that. We all know that," he said as he rubbed a hand up and down her arm.

Okay, enough of that topic for now. "You said something about love?"

He held her a little tighter. "First, you need to know I'm still angry."

She nodded, but she couldn't fight the hope building inside her. She'd been slammed from one end of the spectrum to the other, ever since he'd shown up at her door weeks ago. Now her heartbeat kicked up again.

"Got it."

"But yes. I'm about two steps away from being irretrievably in love with you. Right now I'm *mostly* irretrievably in love with you."

She tried to swallow her smile. Tried and failed. "Two steps, huh?"

"If you keep things from me, it's going to take longer to get there."

She rolled her eyes at him because…really. "Okay, you made your point."

"Then get this." He kissed her cheek, then her chin. "You wind me up and spin me around. I love verbally sparring with you. I love the quiet times. I really love the bedroom stuff." He stopped and took a long breath. "But, mostly, I love you."

Her fingers slipped into his hair. She couldn't get close enough. "That's ridiculously romantic."

"I want you to stay here. Build the estate with me and help me win over my brothers."

That sounded so permanent. So much like a relationship, a commitment. She'd never dared to hope she'd find that with anyone. With Carter she'd been so careful to guard her heart. He'd talked about running in the past, but this sounded very different.

"What about your dad?"

Carter frowned. "We'll hope he reconciles with Beth and leaves the country."

"Poor Beth."

"I have a feeling we're going to be saying that a lot." His hand slipped up and under the hem of her shirt. "You make me want to set down roots, to be better."

"Carter."

"But there's one thing." His smile faded and he grew more serious. "I know there's a load of baggage between us that neither of us put there. We need to take some time and unpack it. I'm just asking that we do it together."

The last few minutes had been perfect. He'd opened up, confessed his feelings for her when he wasn't totally sure he'd intended to stick around. He took a risk; now she could, too.

He was stubborn and exasperating and so hot and as good as it got. So many amazing characteristics rolled into one. "I love you."

His eyebrow lifted. "You sure? I've been told I can be difficult."

"It doesn't seem to be something I can stop, no matter how grumpy you get."

He nodded as his hand continued to skim over her bare skin. "Ditto."

"What now?" She asked, but the fact that his fingers had started roaming gave her a clue.

"We make up."

She couldn't help but tease him since he looked so determined. "Didn't we just do that?"

"Formally."

"Oh, I see." She turned in his lap until she straddled his thighs. "This involves the bed, I presume."

He shrugged. "Those are the rules."

But one more thing.

When he leaned in to kiss her, she put her fingers over his lips. She wanted to be clear one last time. "I am sorry for not sharing more. I promise I'll work on it."

"We'll take our time."

"But you still want me to move in to the main house?" She'd live in a shoe, if he wanted to, but the main house was pretty spectacular. She still couldn't walk into a room without wanting to dust it, but she was pretty sure that sensation would go away at some point.

"Right after we formally make up."

There was that phrase again. She was a fan of the idea. "I like your priorities."

He shot her a sexy smile. "Well, I am the same guy you had a crush on as a teenager."

With a groan she dropped her forehead on his shoulder. "Am I ever going to live that down?"

"I plan to tease you for the next forty years."

Through the joking and the touching and all the talking, she heard the promise in his voice. With other men that might not mean much. With Carter, it meant everything.

She kissed him instead of answering. Let him feel her love and her commitment before lifting her head again. "I'm going to hold you to that."

"Forever."

Yeah, forever.

* * * * *

HARLEQUIN *Desire*

Available October 2, 2018

#2617 MOST ELIGIBLE TEXAN
Texas Cattleman's Club: Bachelor Auction
by Jules Bennett
Tycoon Matt Galloway's going up on the bachelor auction block, but there's only one woman he wants bidding on him—his best friend's widow. Then his plans to seduce the gorgeous single mom get *really* complicated when old secrets come to light...

#2618 THE BILLIONAIRE'S LEGACY
Billionaires and Babies • by Reese Ryan
When tech billionaire Benjamin Bennett returns home for his cousin's wedding, a passionate weekend with his former crush—his older sister's best friend, Sloane Sutton—results in *two* surprises. But can he get past Sloane's reasons for refusing to marry him for the twins' sakes?

#2619 TEMPT ME IN VEGAS
by Maureen Child
Cooper Hayes should have inherited his partner's half of their Vegas hotel empire. Instead, the man's secret daughter is now part owner! The wide-eyed beauty is ill suited for wheeling and dealing, and Cooper *will* buy her out. But not before he takes her to his bed...

#2620 HOT CHRISTMAS KISSES
Love in Boston • by Joss Wood
International power broker Matt Edwards can never be more than an on-again, off-again hookup to DJ Winston. But when he moves to Boston and becomes part of her real life—carrying secrets with him—their red-hot chemistry explodes. Will they finally face the feelings they've long denied?

#2621 RANCHER UNTAMED
Cole's Hill Bachelors • by Katherine Garbera
When wealthy rancher Diego Velasquez donates one night to the highest bidder, he's bought by a nanny! But after one fiery encounter, beautiful Pippa slips away, driven by secrets she can't reveal. Now this Texan vows he'll learn the truth and have her back in his arms!

#2622 THE BOYFRIEND ARRANGEMENT
Millionaires of Manhattan • by Andrea Laurence
Sebastian said yes to Harper's fake-boyfriend scheme—because he couldn't resist! Now, as her date at a destination wedding, every dance, every touch, every kiss makes him want more. But when a blackmailer reveals everything, will they choose to turn this false romance into something real?

HDCNM0918

Get 4 FREE REWARDS!

We'll send you 2 FREE Books plus 2 FREE Mystery Gifts.

Harlequin® Desire books feature heroes who have it all: wealth, status, incredible good looks... everything but the right woman.

FREE
Value Over
$20

YES! Please send me 2 FREE Harlequin® Desire novels and my 2 FREE gifts (gifts are worth about $10 retail). After receiving them, if I don't wish to receive any more books, I can return the shipping statement marked "cancel." If I don't cancel, I will receive 6 brand-new novels every month and be billed just $4.55 per book in the U.S. or $5.24 per book in Canada. That's a savings of at least 13% off the cover price! It's quite a bargain! Shipping and handling is just 50¢ per book in the U.S. and 75¢ per book in Canada*. I understand that accepting the 2 free books and gifts places me under no obligation to buy anything. I can always return a shipment and cancel at any time. The free books and gifts are mine to keep no matter what I decide.

225/326 HDN GMYU

Name (please print)

Address   Apt. #

City   State/Province   Zip/Postal Code

Mail to the **Reader Service:**
IN U.S.A.: P.O. Box 1341, Buffalo, NY 14240-8531
IN CANADA: P.O. Box 603, Fort Erie, Ontario L2A 5X3

Want to try two free books from another series! Call 1-800-873-8635 or visit www.ReaderService.com.

---

*Terms and prices subject to change without notice. Prices do not include applicable taxes. Sales tax applicable in N.Y. Canadian residents will be charged applicable taxes. Offer not valid in Quebec. This offer is limited to one order per household. Books received may not be as shown. Not valid for current subscribers to Harlequin Desire books. All orders subject to approval. Credit or debit balances in a customer's account(s) may be offset by any other outstanding balance owed by or to the customer. Please allow 4 to 6 weeks for delivery. Offer available while quantities last.

Your Privacy—The Reader Service is committed to protecting your privacy. Our Privacy Policy is available online at www.ReaderService.com or upon request from the Reader Service. We make a portion of our mailing list available to reputable third parties that offer products we believe may interest you. If you prefer that we not exchange your name with third parties, or if you wish to clarify or modify your communication preferences, please visit us at www.ReaderService.com/consumerchoice or write to us at Reader Service Preference Service, P.O. Box 9062, Buffalo, NY 14240-9062. Include your complete name and address.

HD18

*When tech billionaire Benjamin Bennett returns home
for his cousin's wedding, a passionate weekend with his
former crush—his elder sister's best friend
Sloane Sutton—results in two surprises. But can he get
past Sloane's reasons for refusing to marry him
for the twins' sakes?*

Read on for a sneak peek of
The Billionaire's Legacy *by Reese Ryan,
part of the Billionaires and Babies series!*

Benjamin Bennett was a catch by anyone's standards—
even before you factored in his healthy bank account.
But he was her best friend's little brother. And though he
was all grown-up now, he was just a kid compared to her.

Flirting with Benji would start tongues wagging all
over Magnolia Lake. Not that she cared what they thought
of her. But if the whole town started talking, it would
make things uncomfortable for the people she loved.

"Thanks for the dance."

Benji lowered their joined hands but didn't let go.
Instead, he leaned down, his lips brushing her ear and his
well-trimmed beard gently scraping her neck. "Let's get
out of here."

It was a bad idea. A really bad idea.

Her cheeks burned. "But it's your cousin's wedding."

He nodded toward Blake, who was dancing with his

bride, Savannah, as their infant son slept on his shoulder. The man was in complete bliss.

"I doubt he'll notice I'm gone. Besides, you'd be rescuing me. If Jeb Dawson tells me one more time about his latest invention—"

"Okay, okay." Sloane held back a giggle as she glanced around the room. "You need to escape as badly as I do. But there's no way we're leaving here together. It'd be on the front page of the newspaper by morning."

"Valid point." Benji chuckled. "So meet me at the cabin."

"The cabin on the lake?" She had so many great memories of weekends spent there.

It would just be two old friends catching up on each other's lives. Nothing wrong with that.

She repeated it three times in her head. But there was nothing friendly about the sensations that danced along her spine when he'd held her in his arms and pinned her with that piercing gaze.

"Okay. Maybe we can catch up over a cup of coffee or something."

"Or something." The corner of his sensuous mouth curved in a smirk.

A shiver ran through her as she wondered, for the briefest moment, how his lips would taste.

Don't miss
The Billionaire's Legacy *by Reese Ryan,*
part of the Billionaires and Babies series!

Available October 2018 wherever
Harlequin® Desire books and ebooks are sold.

www.Harlequin.com

"What's the worst that could happen?" Wyatt asked.

I could get hurt.

Except Lindy didn't need anything from Wyatt. Nothing but his body, anyway. If, in theory, she were to give in to their attraction. He couldn't take anything from her. Not her house, not her land. And if she didn't love him, he couldn't take her self-respect, he couldn't take her heart, and he couldn't give her any pain.

Really, what was the point of going through the trauma of ending a ten-year marriage if you didn't learn something from it? If she knew this was only going to be physical, only temporary...

What was the worst that could happen?

"I..."

He leaned in, his face a whisper from hers. And oh... The way he smelled. Like sunshine and hay. Hard work and something that was just him. Only him.

She wondered if he would taste just the same.

She was about to find out, she knew. He was leaning in, so close now.

She wanted... She wanted to kiss him.

She wanted to kiss another man, finally. To take that step to move on. But more than that, she wanted to kiss Wyatt Dodge more than she wanted to breathe.

And bless him for taking the control. Something she never thought she would think, ever. But he was going to take the decision away from her, and she wasn't going to have to answer his questions, wasn't going to have to do a single thing other than stand there and be kissed.

She was ready.

He squeezed her chin gently, pressing his thumb down on her lower lip, and then he released his hold on her, taking a step back. "Think on it," he said.

"I… *What?*"

But he was already moving away from her. "Think on it, Lindy," he said, turning around and strolling away from her.

She looked around, incredulous. But the street was empty, and there was no one to shout her outrage to.

And damn that man, she still wanted him to kiss her.

***

Good Time Cowboy
by New York Times *bestselling author Maisey Yates,*
available September 2018 wherever
HQN Books and ebooks are sold.

www.HQNBooks.com

PHEXPMY0918